LOSERS

LOSERS

AUBREY MALONE

PENNILESS PRESS PUBLICATIONS
Website:www.pennilesspress.co.uk/books

First published September 2020

© Aubrey Malone

The author asserts his moral right to be identified as the author of the work.

ISBN 978-1-913144-20-3

There's nothing wrong with being a loser. It just depends how good you are at it.

Billie Joe Armstrong

One

It's a night in the spring of long ago and I'm lying in bed waiting for sleep to come. The cinema lights glint from across the street. Down the road I hear the sound of a band playing out of tune at the local hop. I've been at it earlier. I danced with a girl whose eyes were like the sea. I think of her as I look out the window, as I listen to the sounds drifting up to me.

There are voices raised every now and then. People pass the door. There are sounds of laughter and tears, greetings and farewells. The cacophony blends into the music like a counterpoint, rising to a crescendo and then drifting away again until the street is as quiet as a graveyard.

I hear the sound of an Everly Brothers song coming from an old juke-box like some long-forgotten memory. They're singing about weekend passes, ebony eyes, a woman who died on Flight 1203. My eyes well up with sadness for someone I never knew.

It's the time of the night when arrangements are made and phone numbers taken, the time when hopes are raised and lies embellished to hide the embarrassment of commitments half-made in the heat of the moment and subsequently relinquished.

I look at the poster of Elvis Presley on my wall. Further off is the cold grey light of the moon. The wind is blowing softly, the rain making a sound like the crushing of plastic.

I've had a good day but my chest is heaving. My heart is going like a drum. I keep thinking of what I have to face in school tomorrow, of a double period with Creeper. He's the priest who teaches us geography and history. We call him that because of the way he slithers along behind you. I was aware of him at the hop, the inky black of his soutane like a conscience at my shoulder. Was it him or just my imagination? He's haunting my every waking thought. And even my every sleeping thought.

When I fall asleep I dream of him. He appears behind me as I dance with the girl. He's waving a Bible in my face. Has he an obsession with me? Maybe it's me that has the obsession with him.

My dream moves away from the hop. He's in the college now, the college that gives me a lump in my stomach every morning as I cycle down to it. When I get there he's waiting for me. He pulls me into his office and locks the door behind him as he throttles me. Then he drags me to the classroom. He bears down on me, raining blows on my head as the rest of the class watches in silence. They're half afraid they'll be next.

I wake up in the middle of the night in a sweat. Then I realise it didn't happen. I fall asleep again. This time I don't dream.

The following morning my mother knocks on the door. There's a cold sun slanting through the window. I don't know what day it is for a moment. Then the realisation dawns.

It's Creeper day. That means an hour and a half of him, 45 minutes of geography from 9.30 to 10.15 and 45 minutes of history from 10.15 to 11 o'clock.

I've only had a few hours sleep. I don't want to go to school but I know she'll make me. I tell her I'll get up in a few minutes. Two minutes is 120 seconds. Sometimes I count all the way up to that number. Other times I go from 120 to nothing. Today I have less time. I go from 20 down. It's like the opposite of counting sheep. I tell myself that when I reach three I'll get up. I go twenty, nineteen, eighteen, and so on down. I usually get up at about eight or nine.

She puts some porridge in front of me when I come down to the kitchen. I can't face it. I put it down the sink when she's not looking.

I go outside. She tells me to be careful cycling down to the college. I take my bicycle out of the turf shed and pack my books. I haven't done my homework for Creeper's classes. There'll be trouble about that. Even when I do it there's trouble. Maybe it makes no difference. If he doesn't get me for the homework he will for something else.

When I get to the college it's 9.35. I'm five minutes late for the geography class. That means two slaps if I show myself. I decide not to. I hide in the cloakroom instead. I hate geography and he knows that.

I have a cigarette in my pocket that Vinnie Melia gave me. He's in Leaving Cert year. According to Creeper he's trying to corrupt the rest of us.

I wonder if I'll smoke it or not. I don't like cigarettes but I like the feeling of holding one in my hand. If we're caught smoking and missing a class it's a double punishment.

At 10.15 I make my way to the main building. I walk across a field where sheep are grazing. Creeper spots me as I get into the quadrangle. It's as if he's been waiting for me. He grabs me by the ear.

'Going somewhere, are we?' he says.

He slaps me on the face. Then he leads me towards the classroom. It's a situation that's been going on for some time now. Why me, I keep asking myself. Why does he hate me so much?

He's from the country, from a parish called Lahardaun. It's on the banks of Lough Conn. Maybe he hates me because I'm a townie. His friends in the class are the farmers' sons, the pupils who grew up in places like he did, remote farmlands where people eked out a living on slender means.

One of them is from Corballa. His father knows Creeper. Another one is from Laughty. It isn't far from Lahardaun. He has a bond with people like that. It's obvious from the way he talks to them. He relates

9

to them as if they're friends of his rather than pupils. If they're boarders it's even better. It doesn't matter if they get an answer wrong in class or even if they don't do their lessons. Any lapse on their part becomes an excuse for a joke.

Some of these pupils will become priests after they leave the college. Others will take over their fathers' farms. Maybe they'll move to England to work on the building sites. They'll eke out livings in places like Kilburn or Cricklewood or Kentish Town. Some of them might venture to America. It's unlikely any will attend university.

They follow him in everything he thinks and does. He responds in kind, monitoring their progress as if they're surrogate children of his. I'm different. He thinks of me as one of the privileged ones, the solicitor's son with the double-barrelled name.

Having a double-barrelled name is unusual. I don't know anyone else with one. It probably rankles with him. My father's pro-British attitudes probably rankles with him too. His ideal world is one where everyone wears a tricolour in their lapel. And maybe a *fáinne*.

He says the prayer he always says before class: 'Dear Lord teach me to be generous. To give and not to count the cost, to fight and not to heal the wound, to labour and to look for no reward...'

He seems lost in his own world as he recites the words. We follow him parrot-like, not knowing them as well as him but moving our lips as if we do. Even though his eyes are nearly closed we feel he's watching us. He's like a God. Omnipotent and all-seeing.

When the class begins he stands before me. He has that smile on his face that I hate. It's a smile of dominance. He wedges himself between my desk and the one in front of me as he asks me questions. If I can't answer them he pummels me with his fists. It's the way it's been since he first set eyes on me four years ago, the way it will continue until I leave the college. But I've vowed he won't break me. Each time he hits me it only deepens that resolve.

When he gets bored hitting me he asks me why I was late for class.

'I slept it out,' I say. That gets me another punch in the shoulder. This is his favourite stroke. It's like the jab of a boxer.

'That's a lie,' he says. 'You were at the hop, weren't you?'

There's no point denying it. He has his spies everywhere.

'Yes,' I say. He smiles again.

'I'm glad you told the truth. I saw you going in.'

It might be true or it might not be. It doesn't matter.

'Did you hear all the records in the Top Ten,' he asks me. It's the pagan influence from across the water.

'Yes.'

He nods.

'You'd be better off concentrating on the Ten Commandments.'

Everyone laughs. He's got them on his side.

'I suppose you were in the Hibs as well,' he says, 'with the other wasters.'

He's talking about the Hibernian Hall. It's where I play snooker. It isn't only hops that are the sign of a mis-spent youth. Snooker is as well. Especially for me, a boy from a respectable household with a brother already in the priests.

'No,' I say, 'I wasn't.'

'Don't tell me more lies,' he says, raising his voice.

I get a punch in the stomach for each syllable. Don't. Tell. Me. More. Lies.

'So you'd prefer to be a snooker player than a historian,' he says.

I look at the ground. He puts his hand under my chin. He lifts it up.

'A snooker player,' he says again. 'A professional snooker player from Ballina, County Mayo. That would be a nice way to put us on the map, wouldn't it?'

When I say nothing I get another punch. He sees he isn't going to get anything out of me. He becomes bored.

'Okay,' he says, 'Sit down.'

It's the end of Round One.

He goes back to the blackboard. It's full of chalk from yesterday's class. He hands the duster to one of the country boys. They love getting jobs like this. It breaks the monotony.

When the blackboard is clean he draws a map of Ireland on it. He adds Xs to it for some key locations. It's only a sketch but you'd immediately know it's Ireland. He starts to talk about some battle that happened long ago, one of those uprisings where there was a chance Ireland would get help from some foreign country to fight the English. The connection always broke down, he says, either due to a spy's infiltration or lack of numbers or the bad weather causing a ship to be crushed against the rocks upon its arrival on Irish soil. I jot down notes as he talks.

At 11 o'clock the bell goes. My shoulder is throbbing but I'm relieved. It will be another week before we have him for a double period again.

We go out to the handball alley for the break. I try to play with my friend Thomas Glynn but my shoulder is throbbing. He asks me if Creeper hurt me. I say he didn't.

I don't mind him punching me. What I don't like is when he uses his cane. It's made of bamboo. It's broken at the end to make it sting more. Whenever he

12

reaches for it he looks like a swordfighter taking his sword out of his scabbard.

The next class is English. That doesn't give me any problems. My father does most of my essays for me. I give him the titles and he rattles off things that I write down in my copy.

We call the teacher Tag because he's so small. He has to reach up to us when he's pulling our locks.

He was in my brother's class. For that reason he takes a special interest in me. I don't want this. He's always asking me questions about my family in front of everyone else. That bothers me. Another thing that bothers me is the way he flings my copies down at me like a boomerang after he corrects them. He always puts the same question at the end of them all: 'Did you write this yourself?' The answer is no but I don't tell him that. Sometimes he reads the essays out to the class. I'm always embarrassed when he does that. They're far too advanced for my age. Everyone knows I couldn't have made them up myself but Tag doesn't seem to mind. If it was Creeper I'd probably get leathered for it.

The bell goes for lunch after the class ends. Thomas asks me if I'd like to go to Cafolla's for chips. I say yes. I'm still thinking about Creeper. He can see that in my face.

'Don't let him get to you,' he says as we walk down the avenue, 'It's only cowards who bully people smaller than them.'

'What has he against me?'

'I don't know. He can't be a happy man. Maybe he's jealous of you. You have your life ahead of you. He's stuck in a building with a lot of people like himself. Losers.'

'Let's not talk about him,' I say. When you talk about someone you give them power over you. They're in your mind even when they're not beside you. I decide not to let him be in my mind when he's not beside me wedged into a desk.

We talk about other things after we get to Cafolla's. Thomas orders a plate of chips for himself. My stomach is rumbling. I don't eat anything.

I try to focus on the future. There's a soccer game coming up in Belleek that I'm looking forward to. Creeper doesn't like us playing soccer. He's big into GAA. We have to play in secret because of that. In the fields of Muredach's only Gaelic football is allowed. It turns us off it just as the excessive emphasis on the Irish language turns us off that. A few months ago my father wrote a letter to him asking for me to be excused from Gaelic. It's another reason for him to hate me. To him it's a betrayal of the great Muredach's players of the past, people like Willie Casey and others. They're like Gods to him.

After Thomas finishes his chips we walk back to the college. We have a Latin class now. The teacher is small. We call him Butty. He isn't a priest. In fact he's a bit of a playboy. I see him around town in his beaten-up Anglia. He's usually entertaining women. They're often very good-looking. I don't know what his secret is. He isn't much to look at himself. Neither does he put much effort into what he wears. He dresses in suits that look as old as the car.

He isn't able to control us. We make fun of him. Thomas has a way of twisting his hands around his waist to make him look as if he's kissing a girl. When he stands with his back to you it looks as if his arms are the girl's ones. Butty knows what he's up to. He blushes when he looks at him. 'Don't be childish, Glynn,' he says to him.

'Open your books,' he says, 'Page 44. The Punic wars.' He always puts on a defeated expression when he's giving us instructions. It's as if he knows we're not going to obey him. Instead of opening the books we giggle.

14

He beats us when we do that. We all get it. That makes it seem not so bad. It isn't like in Creeper's class where I'm singled out. He's a brute but a laughable one. We run away from him when he starts to attack us. It's like playing Tig except you get a belt instead of a tip if you're caught. Sometimes the headmaster comes in if there's too much noise. When that happens we know we've won. He pretends to give out to us but it's really Butty he's giving out to.

He's the weak link in the chain of teachers in the school. Sometimes I feel sorry for him. A lot of complaints are made about him by the parents when their children come home black and blue. The only ones who don't complain are the parents who beat their own children. There are many of these. Maybe it's easier for their children to be in school than it is for me. For them the college is just an extension of their home lives. My parents never raised a finger to me. But I'd still prefer Butty to Creeper.

He reminds me of what happens to my sisters. They go to the Convent of Mercy. It's not too far from our house. They don't get hit but they get a lot of sarcasm. They say that's worse. I agree. I never know what people mean when they say, 'Sticks and stones may break my bones but names can never hurt me.' Names hurt more than anything.

When the bell rings for the end of the day I cycle home. It's like getting out of jail. Half three on Wednesday is my favourite time of the whole week. It means it's six days before we have Creeper again. I can savour every minute of that time. Cycling across the bridge is almost like being on holidays. On the sunny days I get off the bike and watch the fishermen on the Moy. If it's windy I stay there for ages, opening my mouth wide and inhaling the air into my lungs, expelling Creeper like an exorcism.

When I get back to Arthur Street my mother has a snack waiting for me: a cup of tea and a chocolate sandwich. Usually I wolf it down but today I can't. My stomach is still rumbling.

'What's wrong with you?' she says, 'You've never turned down a chocolate sandwich before.'

I can't tell her about Creeper. It would bother her. She worries more about me than about anything happening in her own life. It's always been the way.

'I had something in Cafolla's,' I say.

She throws her eyes to heaven.

'Junk, probably,' she says. 'You'll get yourself into bad health eating that stuff. If you do, I'll have to bring you down to Dr Igoe.'

He's our local GP. He lives in a big house on the corner of Bury Street across the road from the font. We have a saying about him: 'I go, you go, down to Dr Igoe.' He's a kindly man who never says much. We know we can trust him. He gives my mother pills to relax her when she's stressed, yellow ones that have just come on the market. They have the word Roche written on them. She told me one day they were like miracle pills. They changed her life.

I go into the sitting-room. My sisters are in there doing their homework. They have their copies spread all over the floor. They'll stay like that till after tea. They laugh as they study. It's not like the college where everything is serious. When I do my homework I can't think of anything else until it's finished. Every time I make a blot on the page I think Creeper is going to hammer me for it. They're more relaxed. They make studying a part of their day. It's almost like a hobby to them.

I put the snack back in the fridge. Maybe I'll have it later if my stomach settles down.

I go out to the backyard. One of my brothers is playing golf. It's a little course we've made on the clay. The golf ball is a marble. The club is the handle of a sweeping brush.

16

My other brother is dressed up as Batman. He's making up a sketch based on the TV programme of the same name. He says I can play Robin. He's always making up sketches and putting us in them as the characters. We dress up in costumes from an old wardrobe upstairs. We pretend we're the characters. Or else we play characters from films and mouth the lines. It's like our own Hollywood in miniature in the backyard of Norfolk.

Norfolk is the name of our house. It's in Arthur Street.

At teatime I go down to the Royal Café in Garden Street. That's where my friend Joe Padden lives. His family own it. It's off Lowther's Lane. We swap comics. He usually has Kid Colt ones for me. They're my favourites. People think Kid Colt is a murderer but he's good behind it all. He has fair hair. He dresses in a red shirt with a black and white waistcoat. It's made of thick material like cowskin.

Joe has photos of soccer players as well. You get them inside packets of chewing gum. Sometimes you don't get the photo. You just get an address you have to write to for it. It's in England. I always feel strange writing to England. There are loads of letters after the places' names. One time I wrote away for Danny Blanchflower. I couldn't look at the photo afterwards without smelling chewing gum in my mind.

I make my way over to Thomas Glynn's house. His back door opens out onto the lane. He's interested in my comics but not as much as I am. I tell him he can read them when I'm finished if he wants. I ask him if he'd like to come up to my house to play table tennis. He says he would.

It starts to rain as we walk up to the house. 'Soon it'll be bucketing down,' he says.

We break into a run. When we get to the house I throw my comics under the stairs. We go into the

17

dining-room. It's my father's office now. He's there most days looking through files.

Many of his clients are farmers. Some of them just want something signed. He's only with them a few minutes. As well as being a solicitor he's a Commissioner for Oaths. This means he can sign things other solicitors can't. He only gets a small amount of money for this. He always brings a Bible with him when he's doing it. I don't know why. Maybe the farmers have to swear an oath or something. My mother usually acts as his witness. He says she knows so much about the law she could put a plate outside the door. She could set up on her own if anything happened to him.

There's a safe in the corner of the room. It has all his files in it. If one goes missing it's like a national emergency. Nobody is allowed leave the house until he finds it. One day when I was young I took the key out of the safe and hid it in the garden. Everyone became distressed until I led them out to where I'd buried it. I must have only been about four at the time. I was like the Pied Piper of Hamelin with everyone following me to my hiding place.

My father comes out. He's dressed in the same striped suit he always wears. He has a grey waistcoat inside it.

'You're home,' he says. 'Is it that time already?'

He puts in his monocle to check his watch. He keeps it in a pocket in his waistcoat. After he looks at it he puts it back into the pocket. He opens his eye wide to let the monocle fall out. He never uses his hand to take it out.

He gives me some money. There are always coins jiggling around in his pocket. One day he gave me a penny that had 1961 written on it. I was fascinated by the fact that it looked the same upside down. Would that make it valuable? I didn't know whether to keep it or spend it.

'How did school go?' he says.

'Fine.'

'There's a film in the Estoria tonight if you want.'

I've seen it advertised in the *Western*. It has Forrest Tucker and Rosalind Russell in it. I want to go but I get to thinking Creeper might be there. If he is he'll give me stick about it tomorrow even though we don't have him for any classes. He'll nab me in the playground and start going on about it. He'll start talking about the evils of Hollywood and how films give us all the wrong values about things.

'I don't think so. I have homework to do.'

'I never saw you putting homework before a film before.'

I don't go to the film but I still feel under Creeper's spell the next day. It's as if he can read my mind, as if he's trying to work out how he'll stop me having a life outside him. Seeing him blocks out all the good things that happened the day before, the football and the table tennis game and swapping the comics and talking about things with Joe Padden. It's like a duel to the death between us, a war only one of us can win.

Two

We left Ballina in 1969. Our house was converted into a community centre afterwards. The family went to Dublin, moving into a house in Iona Villas in Glasnevin. Some of my brothers and sisters had been in flats in Dublin since doing the Leaving Cert. They joined us in the Villas now. It became like a Dublin Norfolk. I told myself I had the best of both worlds, the facilities of the city and my family from Ballina. My father often said he wanted to get away from the town so much he didn't care what kind of a house we had in Dublin. That changed when he saw it. He thought it was tiny. 'We should join the house next door onto it,' he said, 'to make it a decent size.' My mother had to explain to him that space was at a premium in Dublin.

The school I went to in Dublin was a posh Jesuit college called Belvedere on North Great Georges Street. It was a lot different to Muredach's. Some of the pupils had been there almost since the cradle. It had a Primary School attached to it too. It was difficult to get into, especially if you were only going to be there for a year like me. My brother Clive pulled a few strings to get me in. A Jesuit himself, he was home on a visit from Africa where he was on the missions. My father looked on it as good timing.

We were encouraged to speak our minds in Belvedere. That made me uncomfortable. I didn't have any opinions on anything. Four years of transcribing my father's essays had turned any ideas I might have had into sawdust. I clammed up if I was asked to give a view on the most straightforward subject. Some of the classes were more like discussions than lectures. If I was asked a question I usually started stuttering. It was a different kind of pressure to the kind Creeper gave me.

My father was glad for me to be in a place with such august traditions but such things meant nothing to me. I didn't make any effort to mix with the other people in the class. They were 'Dubs' pure and simple – or impure and simple – and I was a country lad determined not to shake off my roots. It didn't matter to me that I was walking the same corridors inhabited by people like Ireland's great literary hero James Joyce.

One of the priests teaching us, Fr Brown, had roots in Ballina. He took a special interest in me, trying to ease my path into the new culture. He tried to get me to play rugby but I resisted. The game was as enshrined in Belvedere's traditions as much as it was in any of Dublin's other prestigious colleges but I just didn't like it. It reminded me of American football with all its interruptions. I still preferred the pleb game of soccer. Muredach's GAA was gone but what replaced it was even worse.

I was still outside the loop. Someone said rugby was a thug's game played by gentlemen and soccer a gentlemen's game played by thugs. If that was the case, I preferred to be a thug.

I refused to read *The Irish Times* as well. That was another part of the prestige packet you were meant to lap up. I found it as boring as rugby – and as boring as my classmates. When I listened to the accents of some of them I felt as if I was in an English public school. Many of them were the sons of professional people like doctors and lawyers. So was I but it was a bit different having your father work in the front room of a house in a small town in Connacht than in a five-bedroomed house in Foxrock. I'd have preferred to lie in Foxford than Foxrock. Maybe I had more in common with Creeper than I realised.

Nobody in Belvedere expressed much of an interest in where I came from. Why should they have? One day the English teacher said, 'Ballina – nice town.' He was correcting an essay I wrote at the time. He didn't look up from the copy as he spoke. That's the only time I remember the town being mentioned in the whole year. He then threw my copy at me. It was the same way Tich used to throw it in Muredach's. It must have been something they taught English teachers in training college. Throw copies at the pupils to stop them getting notions about themselves.

My father didn't write my essays for me anymore. If he had, I doubt they'd have been read out. The competition was too strong. Many of these people would be on our television screens in the years to come. They'd be lecturing in our universities and standing in government offices. They used words like 'epitome' and 'quintessence' in their essays. I wasn't sure what such words meant. Nor did I want to.

They had no fear of authority. In the schoolyard they talked of events of the day, heaping scorn on politicians who were wrecking their world. Like most Dublin teenagers they knew it all. They spoke of Ireland's archbishop, John Charles McQuaid, with a mixture of amusement and disdain. He was the 'epitome' of conservatism for them. To that extent all he deserved was censure. He struck fear into the hearts of many people twice their age in the outside world but for this breed he was just 'John Charles,' a deluded reactionary. They spoke of him with a kind of bemused condescension.

Some of them gave cheek to the teachers. I remember a priest saying to a pupil called Johnny Wade one day, 'I don't like you very much, Wade.' Johnny replied, 'The feeling is mutual, Father.' If someone said anything like that in Muredach's he'd probably have been expelled. In Belvedere all that happened was that everyone laughed. The system was too civilised for corporal punishment. The pampered children of the rich were let run riot until the day when they'd take silk, or ride the big aeroplane to foreign climes to make their fortune.

A few of them drove into class on motorbikes. My brother Basil was going to America to take up a position in General Electric. He kindly gave me his Honda 50 before he went. It was in great condition. He encouraged me to bring it into 'Belvo' but I was too shy to do that. I didn't want to attract any attention to myself. It was easier to crawl into the woodwork. All I wanted was to get a piece of paper under my arm called the Leaving Cert and see where my life took me from there.

'You'll never make friends if you don't play rugby,' Fr Brown said to me. I resisted telling him I didn't want to be friends with the kind of people I saw in the class. That was probably 'mutual.'

Most days I took the bus in. If I was up early enough I walked. I went down Iona Road and up over the iron bridge at Clyde Road that led you to Dorset Street. It wasn't too far from there. I wasn't nervous going into school anymore but I felt sick for another reason – pollution. The foul-smelling canal was a poor substitute for the gently rolling Moy.

In the middle of the year we were sent on a retreat to Manresa House. It was a Jesuit centre of spirituality on the Howth Road. Everyone trooped in like (Father) Brown's cows. We felt very sophisticated as we contemplated why we were put on the earth. Everyone sat around discussing things like Liberation Theology. It was all very civilised. 'I don't believe in going into a church to pray,' one of the guys in a tweed jacket said, stroking his chin like Jean-Paul Sartre, 'I do it better walking down the street.' I wasn't sure how Creeper would have taken that.

Some days instead of coming home I went into the Cosmo snooker hall in O'Connell Street. It was a rough place. There was a fruit machine at the entrance. One night I saw a man pulling it down on top of himself. It's a miracle he wasn't crushed to death. Obviously it wasn't paying out enough money. Fights broke out on other nights. It was nothing to hear the siren of an ambulance outside and men in white jackets rushing in to stop someone bleeding. One night when I was in the middle of a game a man got out from under the table and proceeded to comb his hair. Obviously he'd been asleep there for a few hours. He stood up as cool as you like and started admiring himself in a mirror. He looked like a homeless person.

I mainly played with out-of-work taxi drivers and journalists. They were usually between shifts in the nearby offices of the *Irish Press* and the *Irish Independent*. I liked getting to know them. There were a lot of hustlers in there. Some of them would have sold their grandmothers down the river to score a point. The taxi drivers were the worst. They had all the time in the world to practise. They let you win a few games and then played you for money. At that stage their real skills came out. I felt like Paul Newman in *The Hustler*. If you complained you'd get your thumbs broken.

Once I got to know them they stopped trying to win money from me. We almost became friends. The Cosmo became as important to me as the Hibernian Hall had been when I was in Ballina. Some nights I wandered out of it in the middle of the night. The streets would be empty as I walked home except for a few stragglers who looked like they'd knife you as soon as look at you. I often saw the next morning's milk already on the doorstep as I got to Iona Villas. My mother said, 'You're turning night into day.'

I got a good Leaving Cert despite all the hours I lost playing snooker. I'd done the 'Matric' as well. It was a kind of back-up. It enabled me to get a scholarship to the university. Being the last of five brothers meant I needed one. Money wasn't flush.

The other four had gone to university too. That put a strain on my father.

He wanted me to go to Trinity College. He'd been there himself to study law back in the 1920s. At that time it was regarded as a sin for a Catholic to go to Trinity. Now it was almost seen as a sin not to, at least if you were 'well got.' Whether I was or not, I preferred 'National,' as he called it, to TCD. He thought I'd run into 'Mickey Mud and Paddy Stink' there, to quote Joyce. I told him I'd prefer them to Hotsnot Harry and Snooty Sam.

The campus had recently moved out of Earlsfort Terrace. It had been re-located to a stretch of land in a place called Belfield in Stillorgan. I was sad about that. I'd been looking forward to going in to 'The Terrace.' It had history attached to it. I thought Belfield would be bland by comparison. I imagined it having the airy emptiness of modernity.

I was right. In many ways it was like an extension of Belvedere. The lecturers didn't really bother with me. Most of them didn't know who I was. Nobody cared what time I went into lectures at or even if I went in at all. They weren't aware of any of us. You either took down notes or you didn't. It was up to you.

I enrolled for a B.Comm. I was good at Maths. People made the deduction that this would make me a good accountant – and rich. It seemed to make sense. Except for the fact that I hated every moment of the course.

I scraped through the exams. That summer I went to London to be a barman in an Irish pub in Finsbury Park. On my days off I spent most of my time drinking on the other side of the counter. One night after having six glasses of bitter someone said to me, 'You don't sound like an accountant.' That was good enough for me. When I came home I switched to Arts.

I took English and Philosophy as my subjects. Everyone else had to do three subjects but I got an exemption in Maths from the Commerce year. It had that benefit at least.

Some of the philosophy lecturers were priests. It was the last thing I expected. The students made fun of religion. One of the people in the philosophy class was training to be a priest. He was studying theology in Clonliffe as well as being a university student. He was very devout. If you were talking to him and the bell went for The Angelus he'd stop talking in mid-sentence and launch into it. This usually made people crack up laughing. I wondered how Creeper would have dealt with the situation. I didn't think he'd have been taking out his bamboo stick to reprimand him. If he did he'd probably have been impaled on it.

The thinking on sex was casual as well. On Valentine's Day free condoms were given out in the Students Union shop. My Clonliffe friend went into a decline about that. He thought he was seeing a reconstructed Sodom and Gomorrah in Dublin 4.

I came out of my shell in the university. The person who'd been stifled by Creeper in Muredach's and by snobocracy in Belvedere was given oxygen in the freewheeling world of Belfield. I bought Bob Dylan records. I went to Fellini films. I read books by Sartre and Camus. I read Norman Mailer, Malcolm Lowry, Dostoevsky. Everything was up for grabs. Sartre and Camus were a long way from the books I'd been reading in my childhood – Sweet William, Biggles, The Famous Five.

Ballina became irrelevant after I settled into Belfield. I felt like someone growing out of a suit of clothes that didn't fit them. I still had a fondness for it but it wasn't an important part of my life anymore. I was full of the excitement of studying Philosophy and English.

Things that were happening in my family took my time off it as well. Some of my brothers and sisters were in other countries by now. There was lots of activity. I didn't have time to think about the past.

In the following years I went on trips to Ballina sometimes during the summer months. Not having a base there made it difficult to be anything but a tourist on such trips. Aunt Nellie was my only real family connection there now.

I don't remember ever staying in her house. She was too eccentric for that but she took offence if you didn't. One time when I was in the town I went up to Tina's house in Fenian Street before visiting her. Tina had come to our house to help my mother out when I was only a few weeks old and stayed with us until we left the town. Aunt Nellie was peeved that I went to see her first. I don't know how she heard about it. People seemed to find out everything about everyone in country towns. In that respect they were like towns in soap operas.

Maybe that aspect of Ballina would have been crippling to me if I'd stayed there. Whether it would or not, I had to forget about it now. I had to forget it like you'd forget everything else you left behind. I succeeded in that, at least as far as I knew. Going back to it made me feel like a murderer returning to the scene of the crime. It was a dangerous passion to indulge. I tried to convince myself the town didn't exist, that it had somehow fallen off the map of Ireland into the sea, never to be heard of again. It became like Mayo's version of Atlantis for me.

Three

My father went back to Ballina in 1975 to contest an old court case that had been dragging on for years. He wanted closure on it. It was about the executorship of a will. The family involved wanted him to give it up but he didn't want to. He had a sentimental reason: it was the will of his first girlfriend. The man who married her wanted his own solicitor to deal with her estate.

He brought him up to Iona Villas to try to persuade my father to give it up. He was going to do that but one day when he went in to meet him for a consultation he got an instinct something was wrong. He always trusted his instincts even if they seemed to be based on tiny details. In this case it was the simple fact of one of the other people in the room reading a newspaper upside down. 'Why would anyone do that?' he said. 'It was as if he was trying to appear casual, to pretend he was reading it.' He came to the conclusion he was trying to hide something.

On a whim I decided to go down to Ballina with him for the case. I was doing an M.A. at the time. People thought of an M.A. as a big deal but to me it was just like an extra year tagged to the B.A., a doss year to save me having to go out into the big bad world of work. Half the marks you got were based on what you wrote in an examination hall at the end of the year and half on a thesis you did. I chose as my subject the writing style of Ernest Hemingway. I was big into Hemingway at the time.

My father didn't share my passion for him. After getting on the train for the west he asked me how the thesis was going.

'Not too bad,' I said.

'Hemingway was a communist, wasn't he?' he said then.

28

'I don't know what he was,' I said. I had a vague idea of his politics from *For Whom the Bell Tolls* but that wasn't my area of interest.

'He's a writer,' I said, 'not a politician. Why should it matter what he was?'

'I was brought up to fear the hammer and sickle.'

'Let's not get into that.'

'I agree. Thanks for coming down with me.'

'No problem. I'm looking forward to it.'

My mother wasn't with us. She didn't see the point of it. She never liked confrontation of any sort.

'You're retired,' she said to him when he told her he was going to fight it, 'Can you not accept that?'

'This is different,' he said to her, 'It's personal.'

He had a brief case with all his files in it. They were bursting out of it so much he couldn't close it properly. The catch was broken. It was the same case he'd used for his work in the sixties. He'd hardly opened it since we left Ballina.

When the train stopped at Manulla junction I went out to get some tea. He hardly saw the cup when I brought it back. He was too busy rummaging through his files. I'd never seen him doing that for any of his cases before.

'Why are you working so hard?' I said, 'Surely you know what's involved by this stage.'

'There are a few grey areas. I'm not sure what they'll throw at me.'

'Why don't you just wing it? You always did that in the past, didn't you?'

'Sometimes I did. It's not that simple. I'm older now. I don't want to make a fool of myself.'

'There's no danger of that.'

'I don't know. I've been away from this kind of thing for a long time now. I've even forgotten the basics.'

He stayed buried in his files for the rest of the journey. I tried to read a magazine but I couldn't concentrate. It made the time drag much more than I'd expected.

I got a lump in my throat as the train pulled into the station. As the steam hissed and the platform came into view the past came back to me in a wave. I felt I was in short pants again. I was taking down the numbers of the trains with Joe Padden, jumping in and out of the carriages.

'What do you think of the town?' I said to him as we got out.

'What I always think of it – that the best thing about it was the road to Dublin.'

We stayed in a small hotel on the Station Road. It was only a short walk from the courthouse. When we got to our room he threw his case on the bed.

'No more work tonight,' he said.

He opened another case that had his clothes in it, hanging some of them in the wardrobe. I did the same with mine.

'Let's have a drink downstairs,' he said then.

As soon as we got into the lounge it became obvious to me that most of the staff knew him. The ones who didn't had heard about him. His reputation cast a long shadow even yet.

It wasn't long before he was entertaining them all with his stories. I'd heard most of these before. Relating them again in front of a crowd adrenalized him. He excelled at making them dramatic. All someone had to do was mention a character from his past and he was off. Listening to him I felt I was back in Norfolk.

He embellished incidents from the old days, getting lost in them the same way he got lost telling jokes or giving out recitations. No matter how many years had passed since the events he was talking about took place he made it seem like yesterday.

He had everyone in howls of laughter. They enjoyed his personality as much as the stories. As I looked at him I saw the man who must have entranced my mother all those years ago.

She was shy when they started going out together. He brought her out of herself. Whenever they went into a crowded room it wasn't long before he made her feel at home. She enjoyed the way he collected people around him. He brought the best out of them in the process of bringing the best out of himself.

After a few hours we went up to our room. Like a lot of performers he became quiet now that we were on our own. I felt he missed the buzz of the crowd. I was a poor replacement for them.

'You're a great man for the stories,' I said to him.

'That wasn't the real me. I do it because it's expected of me. To tell you the truth I'd prefer if people stayed away from me. They egg me on too much. I wear myself out with them.'

I asked him if he'd like to go down to Norfolk.

'No thanks. If I never see that place again it'll be too soon.'

We were so different. I couldn't wait to jog my memory. All he wanted to do was prepare his case. I wondered if I'd have been like him if I'd spent as long in the town as he had. I left him poring over his notes.

Walking down Arthur Street always stirred emotions in me. No matter how much it changed since we left, there was still enough of it the same for me to be able to throw my mind back to the things we did back in the day.

The house looked the same, at least in its structure. It didn't have my mother's riding colours on it. Our old yellow and brown had been replaced by a garish purple.

I looked across the road where the old school used to be. I hadn't gone to it but my brothers had. It was an industrial estate now.

The Town Hall had been turned into an apartment complex. Gildie Ahern's house was an electrical shop. He'd lived two doors up from us. His orchard was gone. We used to steal apples from an orchard he had out the back. One day he chased after us with a pop gun, firing bullets into the air like some old-timer from a film. I grew up fearing him. I now knew he was harmless behind his rough appearance.

I thought of Syron's chip shop, of Fahy's grocery at the corner. The petrol station that used to belong to the Cottrells had a different name. They were good friends of my older brothers and sisters. I was very young when they left Ballina. They went to England. Mr Cottrell was originally from there. His daughter Donna made her own record once, 'Doonaree.' As well as having a haunting voice she was beautiful to look at. My brothers had a crush on her. Anytime she came to the door they'd look across the road at her. If she looked back they'd scamper inside.

The *Western People* was where Geraghty's shop used to be. Aunt Nellie's house on the Killala Road was gone too. It was turned into a petrol station.

Cobwebs blew over the building that used to be the Estoria cinema. The shape of the building was the same but it was a real estate office now.

I stood outside the door of Norfolk. I tried to picture myself back in the past, cast back there in some Time Machine like in the H.G. Wells book. But if I did that it would be as an adult. I'd have been outside the experience, unable to recapture it.

I sat on the window-sill to the right of the door. It was the one we used to sit on when we were waiting for our turn at hopscotch or marbles. There were five windows altogether, three upstairs and two downstairs. It seemed so symmetrical, so well ordered. It was just like our lives were then.

I thought of the song 'On the Street Where You Live' from *My Fair Lady*:

'I have often walked down this street before
But the pavement always stayed beneath my feet
before
All at once am I several storeys high
Knowing I'm on the street where you live.'

It was a love song but it could just as easily have been applied to a place. Maybe you could feel as strongly for a place as you could for a person.

I felt myself being transported to the past. It was June. We were getting off school. I was looking forward to a cowboy film in the Savoy with Dan Duryea. After it I'd go into Syrons for a bag of chips and some onion rings. I'd play with the pinball machine outside the counter as Mr Syron got them ready. Afterwards I'd play backs and forwards up against Mr Leonard's gate.

My father would send me down to Geraghty's to get some things. We never paid in cash. It was always a case of 'Put it on the book.' We pre-dated the credit card era. The 'book' had lots of items on it that I wasn't able to make out because I could never read his handwriting. The prices of the items put down by Mr Geraghty were equally hard to decipher. My father would fix on a figure each month and give it to Mr Geraghty in payment. Neither of them would know it was too much or too little or if it bore any relation at all to what was bought. It seemed to be just plucked out of the air.

Everything became scrambled in my head. I started thinking of how I left the town. Why did it have to be my Leaving Cert year? Why hadn't I been born a year earlier? If I was I could have finished my schooling in Ballina and maybe got a job there.

Why wasn't I still living in Norfolk? Why couldn't I have stayed there instead of in a faceless hotel? Why did my father have to retire?

If I was working in the town we'd never have had to sell Norfolk and move to Dublin. We could have gone on forever playing golf in the backyard and other games in the house. All Dublin had was people trying to be smart. That was my impression of them after I started going to Belvedere. People told me the cream of Ireland went there. I thought of Samuel Beckett's comment: 'Yes, rich and thick.' Deep down they knew nothing. The students in UCD didn't either. They just copied down things that they were told by the lecturers. It was the same as me copying down my father's essays when I was a child.

I wanted to be back to that time now, back swapping Kid Colt comics with Joe Padden and playing football in Lowther's Lane.

I don't know how long I sat on the window sill. It seemed ages. Eventually a woman came out. She looked official.

'Can I help you?' she said. She had her hair cut tight in a bun. For a moment I was going to tell her who I was but then I thought: What was the point?

'No,' I said, 'I was just daydreaming.'

She screwed up her face. What right had she to look at me like that when I was outside my old house? She didn't even own it.

The day darkened. I didn't want to go back to the hotel yet. I knew my father would still be in the thick of his work. I wondered if I should look up someone from my class. What about Joe Padden?

I didn't even know if he was still living in the town. The same applied to most of my other classmates. I hadn't kept in touch with them since I left. I used to see some of them around Dublin every now and then. We'd stop and talk for a few minutes and then part, each of us aware that we didn't really have anything to say to one another now. Ballina was the glue that held us together. When that disappeared, everything else did as well.

The parents of some of the people I knew still lived in the town. It meant they would have had a home to go to during the holidays even if they lived somewhere else. I envied them that. If I saw someone I knew from the old days on a visit to Ballina I'd have to meet them in a café or bar if I wanted a chat. I wouldn't be able to invite them back anywhere.

We'd burned our boats. Iona Villas could never be another Norfolk for me but at least the family were there. That made it into a sort of home. Dublin was the place where I was installed for my further education. It was the place where things happened. But I knew there'd come a time when my life slowed down. At that point I'd start to think of the past again. It would be like a wound. I'd obsess on my childhood, telling myself I'd have been happy to go back to Ballina in a heartbeat to do nothing if we could be in Norfolk again. I'd be like one of Chekhov's 'Three Sisters.'

I decided to go over to the Hibs. If the Estoria was my second home, that was my third one. I used to play snooker there for hours at a go. My father didn't approve of it. He thought it attracted the riff-raff of the town, the 'Mickey Muds and Paddy Stinks.'

How many hours had I spent there trying to pretend to myself that I'd make a snooker player some day? The talent wasn't there but the obsession for the game was. Maybe our obsessions are all that much greater when that's the case. We chase the forbidden fruit.

I thought of the games I played with Sean McDonnell. He was a man who did odd jobs for us. My mother practically adopted him. She practically adopted everyone who came to the house.

He ended up living with us. I used to beg him to play with me but he was usually too busy. Sunday was the only day he could spare. I used to look forward to it for that reason.

He had an unusual playing style. He hit the ball as hard as he could in the hope that if it didn't go into one pocket it might go into another one. Often it did. He got more flukes than anyone I ever knew. We had a saying about lucky people, 'If he fell into the Moy he'd come out with his trousers full of salmon.' That definitely applied to him.

I walked across to the crazy footpath at the font. I went down Bury Street, past Benny Walkin's house and the elaborate greenery of Tomy Burns' garden. I passed the offices of Burke, Carrig and Loftus. When I got to the post office I sat on the window sill and looked down King Street. There were a few new businesses but mostly it looked the same as it always did. There was Gaughan's pub, Moyletts where we sold strawberries, Clarkes where my father sometimes bought jugs of ice cream.

I stood outside The Hibs thinking of all the games I'd played there, of people jumping up on the table when they couldn't reach a shot, of playing sword-fighting with the cues when we got bored with snooker.

I looked in the window. The tables were gone. It was just a big room now. All that remained of the way it used to be was a sign on the wall saying 'Rules of the Game.' How many tales could the room tell if it could talk? How many people like me came back to it pining for it to be the way it used to be? Or was I the only one? Whenever I met the people I used to play with they'd say something like, 'Yeah, it was good crack' and leave it at that. It meant an awful lot more to me than that.

Was that because I no longer lived in the town? Were people only sentimental because they couldn't have what they once had? If they had it all the time would it become inconsequential to them?

It was only six years since I left but it could have been sixty. How could a place I forgot so quickly be so important to me now? Were all my emotions this fickle? Was I capable of thinking something didn't matter to me one minute and did the next?

Maybe life was all about timing. Ballina had nothing to offer me in 1969 so I dispensed with it for the bright lights of Dublin. Such lights now seemed dull. I'd had my fill of the city and everything it had to offer.

Life in Belfield had started to become routine. Ballina suddenly became my town again. Was this loyalty or convenience? Was I looking at it through new eyes because it suited me? Were the old ones more reliable? Mark Twain once said, 'If you fulfil your longing to return to your boyhood town you may find it isn't the town you're longing for but your boyhood.' Was that true for me too?

I walked down King Street. The smell of the Moy hit me as I turned right towards the bridge. A breeze came up from it.

I decided to go down to Muredach's. It wasn't very far away. How often had I crossed this same bridge with a knot in my stomach thinking of what Creeper might do to me? How relaxing it was to approach the college now with nobody to account to or nothing to fear. That feeling in itself nearly made the idea worthwhile.

Because it was summer there were no pupils there. The building looked as commanding as ever but it was showing signs of age. The grass was overgrown around it. The sheep I remembered from my time there weren't visible anymore.

I walked around by the handball alley. It always seemed so huge to me. My brothers used to love it. They played one another all the time. There wasn't much else to do between classes.

I looked in the window of what used to be a classroom. Chairs lay strewn upside down on top of the desks. A priest waved out at me. I wasn't sure who it was.

Would Creeper have been inside somewhere? Would he be preparing for next year's classes? I had no way of knowing. More likely he'd be in Lahardaun. I wondered what I'd say to him if I met him. Probably nothing.

I sat on the grass thinking about him, about the oppressive influence he had on me, how he stole my life away when so many other people around me were trying to make my youthful years fulfilling for me. Was it some need in him to punish people who had more going for them in life than he had? Did it give him some perverse pleasure to project his misery onto them?

Evening was coming on as I walked back to the hotel. I watched shoppers bustling around me as they stocked up for the weekend. I tried to stop thinking as I looked at them. I always thought too much. Thinking never solved anything.

I went up Arthur Street. It looked empty. The courthouse was at the top of it. It was across the road from the font. How many cases had my father won there when he was in his prime? I was too young to have witnessed them at first hand. I wasn't too young now but I didn't want to go to this one. I was always superstitious about things like that. If I went, I told myself, he'd lose. If I didn't, he'd win. It was as simple as that.

I knew how much it meant to him. It wasn't the money. It was his pride. Could he make one last surge for glory? I hoped so. He was slowing down now but he still had the charm, the rhetoric. I felt sure he'd be able to ferret out the nuances that could swing it for him.

It started to rain as I reached the font. I hadn't my overcoat on so I got the full force of it. It was one of those downpours that got right inside you.

When I got to the hotel I was saturated. As I ran up the stairs my clothes were sticking to me. I banged on the door of our room so much I almost knocked it down.

'Is that you?' he said.

'I'm drowned. Let me in.'

He came to the door. He had a file in his hand. His hair was tousled. The monocle popped out.

'Good God,' he said, 'Look at you.'

If it was my mother she'd have pulled my clothes off me. He just laughed.

'I didn't hear the rain,' he said, 'I was busy.'

'Look out at it,' I said.

He went over to the window. It was still pelting. The raindrops were as big as golf balls.

'Get into the shower fast,' he said, 'You'll get pneumonia.'

I grabbed some dry clothes and went into it. My wet ones weighed a ton. I threw them onto the floor and turned the nozzle. The water jetted down on me. The dial was faulty. If you turned it the slightest bit it went from freezing you to burning you to a cinder. I didn't stay inside long.

I was still shivering when I turned the jet off. I wrapped a towel around me and put on the dry clothes. I felt refreshed. That was the great thing about a shower. It gave you energy.

He was still rummaging through his files when I came out.

'I bet you feel better now,' he said.

'You have no idea.'

There was a radiator in the corner of the room. I plugged it in. Slowly I felt the heat coming back into me.

'You were gone a long time,' he said, 'Where were you?'

'I went down to Norfolk. How is the work going?'

'Not too well. It's thornier than I thought. You'd never think there'd be so many files for something like this.'

There was a sea of them behind him. I didn't know how he fitted them all into his case on the train.

'Do you think you'll be able to sift your way through them?'

'I don't know. A lot of them are faded.'

He showed a few of them to me.

'Look at that,' he said as he waved one at me, 'It's the crux of my case and I can hardly make it out.'

He had the monocle back in again. He always looked so serious with it. I tried to look interested but I probably didn't make a very good job of it. He put the page down.

'How does the house look?' he said.

'They've painted it purple.'

I wanted to tell him about it but he didn't seem interested. We were both in our own worlds.

'Would you like to go for a drink?' I said, 'To get you away from the work.'

'That sounds like a good idea. Where would you like to go?'

'I'm not fussy.'

'I'll be with you when I get through this chaos.'

'Don't rush yourself.'

For convenience we decided to stay in the hotel bar rather than looking for anywhere else.

'We could end up in some dump,' he said, 'Or worse, run into one of my enemies.'

I ordered a pint of Smithwicks. He went for a Guinness with a whiskey chaser. It was his favourite combination. He started to relax now that the files weren't in front of him. I felt he'd been over-preparing the case.

He admitted that himself. He said he'd done as much as he could on the ins and outs of it.

'From now on it's in the lap of the gods,' he said, 'I think I know what I have to say but you never know how these things will go. There are too many uncertainties with the law. Usually it's the longest purse that wins. I don't have that.'

He asked me if I'd gone to the Hibernian Hall. I wasn't sure whether to tell him or not.

'Yes,' I said, 'but there's nothing there anymore. Just the four walls.'

I told him I'd been down to the college as well. He seemed interested in that. For a second I was going to go into how I suffered under Creeper but I stopped myself. I'd never brought it up with him before. What good could it do now? It would only have distracted him from what he had to say in court the following day. It would have upset him too much, especially if I said Creeper's crusade against me was probably motivated by him parading of himself like an Edwardian gentleman through the streets of Ballina. You couldn't do that without people wanting to pull you down. He had enough on his plate without me bellyaching about something that went back almost a decade.

I needed to stop thinking about myself. The university had given me a sense of preciousness. It was as if my life was more important than everyone else's. That was the problem with studying philosophy. You tended to brood too much afterwards, to look for skeletons in the cupboard. I'd read a bit of Adler and Jung. Regression therapy was the new holy grail. Ireland was growing psychologists like potatoes. The Famine was over but now we had the famine of the mind.

He'd have been sympathetic if I told him about my childhood traumas but I knew the way he felt about the children that were growing up today. He'd watched enough television programmes featuring spoiled American kids from the Spock generation to

41

know something was seriously wrong with new parenting techniques.

His world was simple. He loved his family and he showed that every day in every way. He didn't expect them to dwell too much on their grievances.

The modern world was coming down with self-indulgence. He saw it in the courtroom dramas he watched on TV. Serial killers were given 'kid gloves' treatment because they said they didn't get enough love in their formative years. They were taken off the breast too early. 'My mother didn't love me.' 'My father walked out.' 'I killed eleven women because I got Rice Krispies for breakfast instead of Kellogg's cornflakes.'

It felt strange drinking with him. When I was a boy I'd seen him in bars when I'd be passing by on the street. He'd usually be regaling people with stories. Sometimes he'd take out a wallet where he kept photographs of the family. He'd show off my mother's beauty and his novena of children to people, pinning them to the wall as he told them our life stories. I couldn't have envisaged joining him in those days in my wildest dreams. Now it seemed right even though I wasn't that much older. We were two men now, talking about all the changes that had taken place for us since we went to live in Dublin.

'Don't think I don't know how much it affected you to leave Ballina,' he said at the end of the night, 'Just because I don't talk about it doesn't mean I don't realise that.'

'It's not your fault.'

'In one way it is. If I hadn't built up debts we wouldn't have had to leave.'

'We'd have left sometime anyway. Don't worry about it.'

His eyes filled up with emotion. He always got sentimental with drink.

'I really appreciate you coming down with me,' he said.

'I did it as much for me as you.'

'I don't care. It's good to have the company. I'm a stranger here now, a stranger in my own town.'

'Do you think I'm not?'

He put his arms around me. He'd never have done anything like that in Dublin. Too much was happening. I only had brief chats with him there, coming from lectures or going to them. Here it was different. There was nothing to distract us.

Both of us drank too much. I fell onto the bed and slept with my clothes on. The next thing I knew it was morning. It seemed just five minutes later.

'You went out like a light,' he said as he woke me up with a cup of tea and a biscuit.

'Drink does that to me. What about yourself?'

'I couldn't sleep. After a few hours I stopped trying. I've been going through my files since dawn.'

'You'll kill yourself with that stupid case.'

'I'm so far into it now I can't go back. It's like being in a river. I'm being pulled by the current.'

'Don't get dragged under. How is your head?'

'Not great. I had too many whiskies. It's always the last one that does the damage.'

'Do you think you'll be able to concentrate in the courthouse?'

'I won't know till I get there. I hope things don't come apart on me.'

'They won't. Stop worrying.'

'I can't help it. It's because it's based on an intricate point.'

'Just do your best. You're spending too much time on it. You always told me not to over-prepare for exams.' Anytime he saw me studying too much he'd say, 'Put the books away. You'd be better off going to the pictures.'

'I'm great at giving advice but not too good at taking it.'

'We're all a bit like that.'

'Will you be coming with me?'

The way he said it, I thought he didn't want me to. Maybe I'd have worked him up. He'd have been trying too hard to impress me.

'I don't think so. I'm not a great fan of courtrooms.'

He looked relieved.

We didn't talk much over breakfast. When we were finished eating I said, 'I'll say a prayer for you in the church.'

'I'll need more than one, I'm afraid.'

In the end I just walked around the town, saying a few prayers on the street instead. I must have been thinking about the guy from Belvedere who'd been on the retreat in Manresa House.

The hours dragged by. I remembered the days when he'd be fighting some case in the past – a man begging at the bishop's palace maybe or someone pulled over for not having a light on his bicycle, the trivial events that seemed so important at the time.

This was different. He was the plaintiff as well as the solicitor. I wasn't sure that was a good idea. There was an old saying in the law, 'He who will be his own counsellor shall be sure to have a fool for a client.' He often quoted it himself.

As the hours went by I began to share his scepticism. On the way down in the train I'd hardly considered failure as a possibility. Now that he'd put the mockers on himself I began to fear the worst. If he lost, what would it do to him? Would he succumb to the depression that hit him sometimes, the depression he tried so hard to keep at bay?

He won in the end. I was over the moon. I had myself so psyched up to believe something was going to go wrong at the last minute I became almost hysterical when I heard.

He was excited too. He made no effort to hide it when I met him on the steps of the courthouse. There were tears in his eyes.

'Congratulations,' I said, throwing my arms around him.

'I can still do it! You should have seen the way I tore them all up on the stand. It was like the old days.'

I couldn't believe he was so high seeing as it was such a small case. Maybe it meant more to him than any big one he'd ever contested. Minor victories taste sweeter to us as we age.

He rang my mother from the hotel as soon as we got in the door. She tried to pretend she was as excited as he was but I knew she wouldn't be. All she cared about was whether he'd do damage to his heart with all the stress. Winning or losing was never as important to her as health. Women were different to men in that way.

We went for another drink in the bar to celebrate. The staff were all there. He'd mentioned the case to a few of them the night before. He hadn't been sure where their loyalties might have been considering they lived in the town. A few of them even knew the man he was litigating against.

He needn't have worried. They were all delighted for him. They wouldn't let him put his hand in his pocket to pay for anything the whole night.

I felt sad as we packed our things the next morning. I couldn't see this situation ever happening again. We'd go back to Dublin and he'd put all the files away and he'd be just a retired man again, not this vibrant presence in a courtroom.

He was quiet on the train. I imagined him re-living the case in his mind, going through every minute of it the way he'd done with other ones when I was growing up. His face looked proud.

The towns drifted by us like chimeras - Foxford, Swinford, Charlestown - all the names I remembered from station platforms on train trips I took to Dublin as a child. They looked so quaint now.

'You'll be dining out on your victory when we get back to the Villas,' I said.

'I'd never have forgiven myself if I lost. I had five years to prepare for it. I probably gave more time to it than all my other cases put together.'

'It was still a great achievement. You were out of practice.'

'I suppose so.'

'Would you consider taking up any other ones now?'

'You mean from new clients? Not if you gave me a thousand pounds. I hate the law and everything it represents. Or should I say everything it *mis*represents.'

He'd always warned all of us away from it as a way of life. For him it centred on the perpetuation of injustices rather than anything else, a succession of mistruths and subterfuges. He used to say 'Lawyer' should be spelt 'L-i-a-r.'

I remembered asking him once what he'd do if a man accused of murder wanted him to defend him. Would he have wanted to know if he was guilty?

'No,' he said, 'I wouldn't want to know. It would be none of my business. The law has no relation to morality. You accept what your client says as the truth and work from there. You don't ask him to take a lie detector test. He either gets off or he doesn't. It's as simple as that.'

When I asked him if he'd like to go back to Ballina to live he said, 'You must be joking.'

'Why?' I said.

'Too many memories.'

I thought: How could you have too many? I even wanted to keep the bad ones. They were all part of the jigsaw.

'What about all your friends?' I said.

He threw his head back.

'They were just drinking acquaintances. Boozing pals rather than bosom ones.'

He'd fallen out with some of them. It was impossible to spend thirty years in a town without doing that. Others had died.

'You can't bring the old days back,' he said, 'It's like trying to fight the tide.'

He said he was tired. All he wanted was to be away from it all. To be with his wife and family as he lived out whatever years remained to him.

Back in Dublin he became restless. A fire had been ignited in him. He'd been stressed worrying about the case for months but it adrenalized him too. What was he going to replace it with?

I didn't have to wait long to find out. He busied himself writing letters to the newspapers, fulminating on the ills of the day, on a world that had gone to rack and ruin in his eyes, a world of lying and cheating and the destruction of all the old values.

Four

My life returned to its routines. I got the 22A bus into Belfield every morning with a happy feeling in my head. It was exhilarating not knowing what was going to happen in the day. Each one was different. A party could come about without notice, or a soccer game, or even a trip down to Wicklow to the Hellfire Club. There was a good pub life after the lectures.

Then there were the dances in the Belfield Craze. Everything was so dark there you didn't even know who you were dancing with half the time. It was an exciting feeling. I rolled out of there some nights hardly knowing who I was, falling into a taxi to get me back to Glasnevin. If there were no taxis I'd cadge a lift with some fellow dissolute.

In the tutorials we engaged in spirited discussions about literature and philosophy. We questioned everything, even the possibility that we didn't exist. Poems were handed to us for us to analyse in every detail like frogs in a laboratory. The word became as important as the world. We lived in glass bubbles of the mind, going into every possible detail of what a writer might have been trying to get at. Meanwhile millions of people died of starvation and natural disasters in other corners of the globe. Such tragedies became discardable in comparison to our rhyming couplets and iambic pentameters.

To stop my brain atrophying I tried my hand at writing. I'd made a few stabs at little pieces in Ballina but they went nowhere. I was too intimidated by my father's rhetoric.

The fact that he did most of my essays for me in Muredach's was crippling to any small creativity I might have possessed. To have a father like I had transcribing essays that would be read out in school the next day was the worst thing that could have happened to me. It made me lazy and inhibited. I'd have been better off struggling with my bad prose like the rest of my classmates rather than being spoiled by plagiarism. It was hard to resist showing off when he was my ghost writer.

There was a page in the *Irish Press* called 'New Irish Writing' that I started to contribute to. It nurtured talents like Neil Jordan and Des Hogan. Both of them went on to become best-selling authors. It was edited by a Corkman called David Marcus.

He expressed an interest in me from the word go. The first story I sent him was one called 'At Lourdes.' I got in trouble with one of my aunts because of it. It was the one who ran a guest house in Dun Laoghaire. My mother was visiting her when it was published. 'Aubrey is making fun of religion,' she said. I wasn't but it could have been read that way.

I didn't know if my mother had been offended by it. If she was she didn't say anything to me. She told my aunt she was cutting her visit short because of what she said. She was steeped in religion herself. I appreciated what she said more than I would have if it came from a non-religious person.

Seeing 'At Lourdes' published lit a fuse in me. Afterwards I couldn't stop writing. Most of my stories in those days were full of angst. My characters were usually too emotionally hyped to be able to go out and buy a pack of cigarettes for themselves. They had everything to live for except a good reason to get up in the mornings.

Even when Marcus sent my work back to me it wasn't with the usual mass-produced rejection slip. He read what I wrote. That wasn't always the case with editors. I knew some writers who stuck two pages of their submissions together to test editors out. You wouldn't fool Marcus with that one.

Sometimes he could be harsh. He sent one story back to me with the message, 'There's less to this than meets the eye.' I think that was one of Tallulah

Bankhead's oneliners. My immediate reaction was to say, 'You bastard.' But after reading the story again I realised he was right.

He published five or six of my stories over the next few years. Sometimes they ran across the whole page. I felt like God on those Saturday mornings thinking half the country was reading me.

Eventually the day came when he asked me to go into his office to have a chat about one of the stories. He was sitting there in a crumpled suit in a dusty little office.

'Your character throws herself off a train platform at eight in the morning in a tiny village,' he said. 'There are about thirty people present. I felt I was reading *Anna Karenina*.' I hadn't known there was a train suicide in that book. Neither had I considered the fact that at that hour of the morning in a remote place there would hardly be more than two people at a train station. Normally I had no time for literary critics. David Marcus was so forensic he changed my view. I began to tailor things to his needs.

He published some of my poems as well. One of the other people in my class was Harry Clifton. He went on to become one of the most respected poets in the country. I might spend six minutes on a poem but Harry could spend six months on one. He was William Carlos Williams and I was Rod McKuen. One day I asked him where he got his inspiration. 'When I'm washing the dishes,' he said. That made me feel a bit better. Maybe William Carlos Williams got his inspiration there too. Maybe Rod McKuen got his inspiration in the Hanging Gardens of Babylon. I tried not to compare myself to Harry. If I did, I'd probably have thrown my hat at writing.

I knew him when he did his first work. I remember him publishing a pamphlet called *Null Beauty*. It was beautiful – the first sign of the caterpillar coming out of the chrysalis. David Marcus was paying us the princely sum of £2 per poem in those days. It paid for a few pints in the Belfield bar.

Harry and myself also did some night security work together to bolster our earnings. Chris Griffin was with us some of the time as well. I'd been with Chris in the Blackstock Hotel. We used to go up to the security office in Mountjoy Square with our clocks and our sleeping bags. We didn't even have to hide them. The boss knew we were going to spend the night asleep. He knew we'd set the alarm for about ten minutes before our relief was about to arrive.

'Don't be a hero if someone breaks in,' he advised us, 'You're just there for insurance purposes.' There was no danger of that. We'd be in the land of nod anyway. We were more likely to be woken up by the mice that crawled up and down our clocks. One night I saw one sitting on a Russian novel I'd been reading. He had good taste. You could do a lot of reading in McCairns Motors or Berger Paints on wet Monday night when there were no distractions, not even burglars.

You could also do a lot of writing. I used to bring copybooks into the huts with me and fill them with all sorts of drivel. Anything I saw was capable of setting me off – a bird in the sky, a cloud formation, a broken bottle on the edge of a footpath. If I saw a discarded high heel on a railroad track I tried to make a story around it, the story of some lost soul on her way home from a disastrous date or someone who missed a train to take her away from a dead life.

Writing meant disengaging yourself from people. I didn't find that too hard to do. I'd never been very sociable anyway. Keith was in the house one night and he asked me if I'd go for a drink with him. He was married at the time. He lived in Artane but he used to visit us a lot in the Villas. Like most of the other members of the family he had to be prised away from home even after he went up the aisle.

51

'I don't think so,' I said, 'I have some writing to do.'

'That's a pity. You're too young to close yourself off from life.'

'It's my choice. What's "life" anyway? I can learn more from a book than a person.'

'Suit yourself.'

He commandeered Hugo instead.

'We're off to the Addison,' he said. The Addison Lodge was a pub he liked. They let you sit forever over your drinks without hassling you.

'Have a good time.'

'We're going to a wedding,' he said, 'I hope you enjoy yourself at the funeral.'

I knew what he meant. I was doing a lot of dark stuff at this time. Maybe good writing had to be dark. Our sweetest songs are those that tell of saddest thought.

There were a lot of people in the house that night. A girl called Marius had come in from next door to talk to June and Audrey. There were other people there as well. I went up to my bedroom. I tried to write but I couldn't. There were people going in and out of rooms all the time and it was distracting me.

I got an idea. I took a six-pack from the fridge and brought it up to the toilet. Then I bought the typewriter up. I put the toilet seat down, put the typewriter on my knee and started typing. Was this the first laptop in Ireland?

I can't remember what I wrote. Probably more drivel with 'less to it than met the eye.' I can't remember how long I was in there either. Anyone with a bad stomach had to grin and bear it that night. There were lots of knocks on the door but I didn't open it until I'd finished my last beer.

Keith and Hugo came home after the pub closed. I was sitting in the kitchen with my prized pages.

'I hope you enjoyed yourself,' Keith said.

'I did,' I said, 'I wrote a new version of *War and Peace*. It'll be out next month.'

'Good for you.'

I didn't know what to do with my M.A. when I got it. People tended to genuflect before you when you had letters after your name but for me they were a sham. I had no respect for the course or for my thesis. I'd have enjoyed it just as much doing one on the history of bus timetables.

I toyed with the idea of doing a Ph.D. for a while but I wasn't sure if my grades were good enough to qualify for it. I asked Denis Donoghue to check but he said he was too busy. He said he couldn't give me 'chapter and verse.' He was rushing off to New York to give a lecture at the time. He did that kind of thing a lot in America. I wondered if they understood him any better over there than we did.

I asked Seamus Deane to check my grades in his absence. After a few months he came back to me. He said I could do the Ph.D. if I wanted but by then I'd lost interest. I had enough letters after my name and they weren't going to be much use to me in the 'real' world. As Keith said, 'You have a B.A. and an M.A. but you don't have a JOB.'

To get away from the dull grind of the books I decided to do some travelling. I didn't care where I went as long as I got away the dull grind of reading. Europe looked good so I decided I'd go there. I didn't pack much more than my toothbrush. I hadn't much money either.

'How are you going to live?' Ruth said to me.

In those days I didn't think much beyond the moment. She was going to Spain for a fortnight with Audrey and Jacinta.

I remember the night they left. They spent an eternity packing. A taxi driver called to the house to bring them to the airport. As he watched them putting their cases into the boot he said to me, 'Are they going there to live?' The man who said 'You can't take it with you' never saw my sisters packing for a holiday.

I linked up with a friend of mine from UCD and we got a plane to Paris. From there we decided to hitch-hike to Athens. We split up every now and then, meeting on and off depending on where we were. It was easier to get a lift if you were on your own.

We did some grape-picking and other odd jobs as we zig-zagged through Europe. It was a bit like the autumn of 1970 with Hugo. I didn't mind roughing it. I slept under bridges and in railway stations. Often I'd get my heels kicked by policemen in the mornings. I kept moving for the sake of it, not staying anywhere long enough to get to know anything about it. I had a friend in Paris who took in post for me. My father sent money to him when I was short. Somehow it got to me. I can't remember what I did a lot of the time.

It was a mindless three months. I was home in time for Christmas.

Five

I wasn't sure what career I wanted to take up. There wasn't much you could do with an Arts degree unless you went into the Civil Service or some PR job. We had a Careers Guidance Officer but he wasn't much good. He just gave you old clichés like, 'If you find a job you like you'll never have to work again.' He had a book called *The Directory of Opportunities for Graduates.* His office had numerous copies of it all over the floor. It was bigger than the Bible. He doled them out to us as if they were going out of fashion. It was as if handing them to us absolved him of the need to do anything else. One of the people in the class used them for firewood in his flat on the Morehampton Road. I was round with him one night when I saw them stacked on the floor like bales of briquettes. He had a fire roaring in the hearth. 'Throw another DOG on it,' he said to his girlfriend. That was his acronym for the Opportunities book.

He didn't know what to do with his future. One theory he proposed was going off to a desert island and playing chess all day. We looked up jobs in the paper but nothing appealed to us, not even potholing in Bogota – though I was somewhat attracted to that. If anyone offered us anything half-decent within spitting distance we'd have chewed his hand off.

An opportunity presented itself from an unlikely source just as we were about to give up hope of ever becoming responsible citizens of our country. John Wilson, the Minister for Education, spearheaded a scheme whereby Arts graduates were allowed to do a one year course in a teacher training college for Primary Teachers. It was St. Patrick's College in Drumcondra. The other students were there for three years. I went for it even though I'd never thought of being a teacher before. There was no ink in my blood, as they said. It was more due to a lack of alternatives than anything else.

My father didn't think it was good enough for me. One of his first girlfriends had been a Primary Teacher. She was a rough diamond. It gave him a bad image of the profession.

'You're made for better things,' he said to me, 'N.T. stands for National Tramp.'

He had me lined up for something like university lecturing. I told him I'd die first. It didn't go down well when I told him I had little respect for that breed. 'They're only eunuchs in the harem,' I said. In the end he gave in. He pretended to be a snob but he wasn't one really.

When I went into Pat's for the first time I felt I was back in Muredach's. There were stained glass windows everywhere. The floors were scrubbed so much you could almost see your face in them. It was a far cry from the plexiglass of Belfield.

I missed the untidiness of Belfield, even the litter strewn all over the corridors. The thinking was different too. Most of the students were conservative. Not many of them looked like they stayed up late at night or missed their three square meals a day.

They thought we were intellectual snobs. Maybe we were. One day a few of them were talking about the TV series *Dallas*. 'Do you follow it?' someone asked me. 'I'm ahead of it,' I said. I don't know what came over me. I wasn't usually so cocky. It bothered me that people knew who J.R. Ewing was but not Jean Renoir.

There was a big emphasis on Irish. We studied it at university level to be able to teach six year olds how to say 'My name is Jack.' It was insane.

Two months into the course we were sent down to a Gaeltacht in Kerry to brush up on our *blas*. Most of the Wilsons among us – we were even naming ourselves after the Minister now - used the time to brush up on our football skills instead. And our capacity for ingesting Smithwicks.

We started to skip lectures. Most days we headed down to the local pub to play pool. It was a pokey little place that looked like it hadn't been cleaned in years. We used to joke that you had to wipe your feet coming out instead of going in.

Word of our forays down there eventually got back to the man organising the trip. He followed us into the pub one day. The proprietor spotted him coming down the *boreen*. He gave us a signal to hide in the snug but it was too late. One of the lads had his cue sticking out and he spotted it when he came in.

He spoke to us as if we were Jews in a concentration camp and he was a Nazi about to gas us. He said if we didn't get back to the lecture-hall immediately we were going to be sent back to Dublin minus the grant we'd been given for the course. That put manners on us – for a few days anyway.

I applied to my old primary school to do teaching practice that winter. It was on the Killala Road opposite my aunt's house. I was accepted but it snowed in December and the roads to the west became impassable. I wasn't able to go down.

I felt fate was working against me. Some things in life just weren't meant to be. I was devastated. I'd really wanted to see how I'd be teaching in my Alma Mater. It would be one in the eye for Creeper. I'd be as good as him or as bad as him.

When Ballina didn't materialise I went to a school in Drumcondra instead. I wasn't sure how I'd fare out standing in front of a class of thirty children. My hair was long in those days. I often went for weeks without shaving as well. You weren't allowed use a razor if you were a UCD student. It was too nerdy. I bought one when I went to Pat's but I didn't use it much. You could easily tell the Wilsons from the diehard Pat's students by the amount of face hair they had.

I saw a cartoon of one of the Wilsons in the *Irish Press* one day. It had a scraggly-haired hippie going into a principal's office with his shirt hanging out and a joint hanging from his mouth. He took the joint out and said to the principal, 'Sixth want to know who won World War II.'

For one of our projects we were asked to come up with unusual ideas to motivate the children. A guy in the class was an electrician's son. He arrived into the college one day with a contraption that looked like a chess board except for the fact that it had a wire and plug attached to it. It had a set of letters on it that you matched to other ones to make words. 'What happens if you match the wrong letter?' the lecturer asked. 'You get a shock,' he said.

I felt I was too quiet to be a teacher. I wasn't a performer like my father. It would have helped if I was. Most of the children I knew weren't interested in school but if you were demonstrative enough you could make a subject come alive.

Why did I become a teacher when I didn't have any particular suitability for it? Maybe for the same reason I joined a dramatic society once - to try and become my opposite. It was also probably the reason I buried the key of my father's safe in our back yard when I was a child. Being the youngest of nine meant I was more used to following than leading. That all changed when I knew something all my elders didn't. It was my first experience of power.

I felt like another Creeper as I stood in front of the class on my first day of teaching practice. I'd jumped over the counter, exchanging the role of pupil for the one of teacher while still being part of the system. Was it a mistake? I didn't know. I kept telling myself I chose the job to undo the damage Creeper did to me. I wanted to make the world a better place than he did, to give the children in my charge a love for learning, a love he all but took away from me when I was under his control. It was coming up to Christmas. The kids were excited. They made me feel good going into them each morning. I felt this might be the right job for me after all.

My father died the following February. He went out like a light with a massive coronary. He hadn't had any symptoms. He'd even brought me breakfast in bed that morning.

He'd been losing his zest for life for a few years now. The world had let him down. Crime and devastation were everywhere. There were no authority figures left anymore, either in church or state. Everywhere he looked he saw chaos. No amount of letters to the paper could do anything to stop that.

He spent a lot of time in his pyjamas. My mother had his bed moved downstairs. That meant she could bring him in cups of tea whenever he wanted them without her having to climb the stairs. He had a bell that he rang when he wanted a cup. It was the closest he came to the grand life he'd always craved, the kind of life he loved reading about in upper crust British novels.

By now he wasn't drinking much. Smoking a pipe became a substitute for it. He'd use half a box of matches trying to light it. He often set the bedspread on fire as he threw the matches towards the grate. He didn't let it bother him when it went up in flames. He'd ring the bell and say, 'The mattress is gone up again.' My mother would come in with a pan of cold water and douse the flames.

As he got older he became more serious. When he told jokes now there was often a bitter edge to them.

He had intimations of mortality. He said he was looking forward to seeing God so he could put him in the witness box for all the misery he'd caused by making the world. 'I'll sue him,' he'd say, 'Let's see how he defends himself in the dock.'

I felt he'd run out of road. He used to quote that line from the song 'Ol' Man River, 'I'm tired of livin' and scared of dyin.'' He spent a lot of time wondering what lay ahead of him in the 'next life.' Most of his friends from Ballina, were probably going to be 'downstairs.' He liked to tell a joke about the gates of heaven being stolen by the devil. St. Peter had to go to hell to find someone to take on the case. That was where all the solicitors were. He felt it would be more fun down there. Heaven for the climate, as he put it, and hell for the company.

I couldn't see his death as a tragedy. It was a release for him. My mother's heart was broken but she knew he went at the right time. Those of us left behind probably suffered more than he did.

I got closer to the other students in the training college. They banded around me and gave me a lot of support. I didn't realise how much I needed it. It was weeks after he died before that I realised how much in shock I was. I'd gone into denial about it. I was glad to have them to turn to. My family were a great solace to me too. Everyone becomes a child when a parent dies. I reverted back to my Ballina bubble.

After I graduated from Pat's I got a job teaching in a small school in Clonsilla. It was Fifth Class. The pupils were all high achievers. I got to know what hard work was that year. They ran me off my feet with their thirst for knowledge but I enjoyed the challenge. Being the youngest of a family meant I hadn't much experience of children. Being a father figure to them was a novelty for me.

I couldn't wait to get into the classroom during my first few years. I enjoyed imparting knowledge and also the other parts of the job – peeling oranges and tying shoelaces.

I refereed football matches after school hours. I took the children to roller discos and sometimes to films. There was no extra money for this. I enjoyed it so much I'd almost have paid to be allowed do it.

It was a few years before the honeymoon ended. I don't know why that happened. Did my enthusiasm trail off or did the routine get to me?

When I took my foot off the gas the children copped it. Nobody is a better psychologist than a child. They started to play up on me. I felt like Butty when they did that. Some of them did their best to wreck my head. When corporal punishment was done away with in 1981 it was like the last straw. I was never in favour of hitting children but it was reassuring to know you could threaten it if things got out of hand. Now you couldn't threaten them with anything.

Once the fun went out of it, the writing was on the wall for me. I started to prepare less classes and to correct less exercises. Eventually I turned into the thing the lecturers in Pat's told us never to become: a clock-watcher.

Six

My mother told me I was spending too much time in the pubs. And too much money. She said I should buy a house to get some discipline in my life. It was the last thing I'd been thinking of. She was practical. Being married to a man who liked a drink would have made her so even if she hadn't been already that way as a farmer's daughter. She didn't want to see history repeating itself. I said I'd think about it.

Sean MacDonnell was living with us at the time. He was the man who organised the auction of our things in Ballina before we left. He said he'd find a good place for me. He always seemed to be around when things were happening. He had a nose for events.

He got into his car one day and we set off. He drove at about a hundred miles an hour. He was always in a hurry, always showing off. We clipped bends, narrowly avoided other vehicles. For a part of the journey we seemed to be on two wheels. My heart was in my mouth.

We ended up in Cabra West. He said that was where the bargains were. He always seemed to know things like that. He had a newspaper with him with the property page open. He'd put biro marks around some of the houses advertised on it, big rings with his scrawly handwriting on them.

We looked at a few but he didn't like any of them. My opinion didn't seem to enter into it even though I was the one who was going to be doing the buying. The roof was wrong. The plumbing looked dodgy. It would need too much refurbishment. He knew it all. He was his father's son.

We ended up in a place called Viking Road in Stoneybatter. The houses were all similar and all made of red brick. They were like the ones you saw in

Coronation Street. None of them had any front lawns. They opened onto the street.

We knocked on the door of one about half way down the road. A man in a T-shirt came out. He seemed to be wearing his breakfast on it. 'Yeah?' he said. Sean said, 'We came about the ad.'

He led us inside. There was an alcove the size of a phone box. I presumed that was the hallway. A second door led us into the house itself.

There was a reasonable sized living room and a little kitchen off it. A woman was cooking something. I didn't like the smell of it. She was a large woman. The kitchen was so small she didn't have room to turn around. Her stomach was touching the cooker and her bottom wedged up against a cabinet behind her. 'Howia,' she said.

The man led us up a staircase. At the top of it there was a landing. It was smaller than the alcove. In front of us was the main bedroom. To the side was a smaller one. A hot press took up most of the space on one wall. It looked out onto the backyard. The toilet was out there. It was behind a wall. There was no bathroom.

The man was looking for £14,500 for it. At that time I had about a tenner in the bank. Sean liked it. When we got outside he said, 'That's the house for you.' I didn't feel the topic was open for negotiation so I said nothing. When we got back to Iona Villas Sean said to my mother, 'We found a place.'

She was delighted. I made a bid of £14,000 for it the next day. The man came down to £14,250 so we took it for that. I got a mortgage for £13,500. My mother paid the rest.

For the first few months it was difficult for me meeting the mortgage. There wasn't much left over from my teaching salary. I'd enjoyed my little time as a spendthrift. Now it looked as if I was going to be back living the life of a pauper again. 'It's an investment,' my mother said, 'It'll stand to you in time.'

Getting tenants was the next step. I put an ad in the paper. There were a lot of calls asking to see it. I arranged a viewing time. When I got there the people who phoned up were already outside the door. They stretched down the street. I let everyone in together. They all seemed to be interested in taking it. I didn't know who to pick. Some of them got aggressive, almost demanding I let it to them. I took their details down in a copybook and said I'd get back to them. Some of them had references. I thought I should give them priority.

I let it to a young married couple. She was very pretty with a pert little figure. He was a quiet man who worked in a meat factory. They seemed like ideal tenants. They were very respectful. 'We'll keep it like a new pin,' the woman said. I believed her. She gave me a month's rent in advance and a month's deposit. She seemed to be organising everything.

She came round to Iona Villas with the rent every month. She was always impeccably made up. My mother used to give her tea. She talked about how she loved the house and the street. She said there was a community atmosphere there. She never had anything with the tea, not even a biscuit. She was too busy watching her figure. She rarely mentioned her husband.

They broke up within the year. I was shocked because they seemed very happy together. Maybe they married too young. I felt sorry for her husband. I knew he was looking forward to being a parent. I don't think she was. Maybe that was why they broke up. She had too much living to do.

A lot of marriages broke up among the tenants in the following years. Many of those in live-in relationships separated too. It was an education for me witnessing such break-ups. I got an insight into worlds I'd never have experienced if I hadn't bought the house. Some of the partings were bitter. Some of them involved broken furniture. People didn't seem to care about things when they didn't own them. Sometimes I got phone calls from the police. There were arguments that spilled out onto the street.

Often I didn't know what kind of people I was putting into the house. They sounded very impressive when they were describing themselves but once they got the keys the balance of power shifted. Now they were the boss, not you. Maybe I wasn't cut out to be a landlord any more than I was to be a teacher. I often fell for sob stories and people took advantage of me. If I got tough with them they were capable of threatening me. One man said he was going to burn the house down. Another one said he was going to go away from it without telling me and leave all the lights on so someone would break in. He was psychologically disturbed.

There were others worse than him. One man took to urinating on the neighbour's door for a thrill. He was on drugs. I went around to him when I heard about it but he wouldn't open the door. It was a long time before I got him out.

Tenants are like every other class of people in life. They look for weakness in the people they're dealing with. They saw a better opportunity for this in my casual attitude to them. I was never cut out for telling people what to do and they saw that. No matter what they wanted I tended to say yes.

One woman asked me if she could paint the living room red. I couldn't believe it when I saw the can. It was the most horrific shade I'd ever seen in my life, even redder than beetroot. I told her she could. If she'd asked me could she paint the roof red I'd probably have said yes.

When she had it done she decided she wanted to leave. A man up the road had a similar house to mine that was cheaper to rent. She was breaking her contract by leaving but I didn't hold her to it. I tended not to do that for the sake of peace. I did it once and the person got aggressive with me. He started threatening me with violence. 'I know criminals,' he said. You couldn't win with people like that. There's an old saying, 'Never get into an argument with someone who has less to lose than you.'

Other people wanted to move furniture around the place. If they had children they wanted a bed in the small bedroom. If they didn't they wanted the bed taken out and a desk or something else put in. I kept taking things out and disposing of them. Then I might have to buy something similar to what I'd just thrown out for the new person. It was a merry-go-round.

I didn't complain. I knew I was luckier than 99% of the population in having the place at all. Michael Caine said once that the secret of life was having something that made money for you while you were asleep. That's what being a landlord is like. Caine often endorses capitalism. Maybe he's entitled to because he came from nothing. I never saw myself as having capitalistic tendencies even though being a landlord has overtones of that. Unlike Caine I never wanted to be rich but I don't want to be poor either. Charles Dickens' Micawber said happiness was when your income exceeded your expenditure by sixpence. It was a view I shared. I didn't need to have money in the bank unless I was saving for something but I tried to avoid being in the red.

I tried to be fair to the tenants. I hoped they wouldn't take advantage of me. If they broke something I told them not to worry about it. Replacing things was cheap if you knew the right place to go. Landlords always know these places. Furniture went for half nothing in them. I got to know them too. Sometimes you'd see other shoppers in them. You'd know they were landlords by the look of them. I hoped I never got that look.

I could see the tenants being surprised by my attitude if they broke something and I acted like I didn't care. They might have been nervous broaching the subject. Some of them would have come from places where the landlord was tough.

I saw the same look in pupils' faces in the school if I was casual when they broke something. They weren't used to that. I was expected to get excited and make a big deal out of it. The parents expected me to get excited as well. The children tended to be more lax at home as well as at school if I didn't.

A pupil stole a pound from a teacher's handbag one year in the school down the road and there was war over it. I found it highly amusing looking at people getting their knickers in a knot over a quid. It was years before I saw the logic of it. If you treated small things like big things there mightn't be any big things.

With me there were always big things. Many tenants left the house looking like a tip. I liked doing it up but sometimes it was in such terrible condition I had to get cleaners in before I could show it to the new people. There'd often be maggots and rotting plants all over the place. There'd be chairs and tables falling apart.

One tenant got his kicks from walking down the street with a chain. After he left I learned he'd been terrorising the neighbours. He used to have vomit-throwing parties on the roof. He left before dawn one morning with a lot of rent owing. There were also unpaid ESB bills and television charges. I couldn't get into the house after he left. The key broke in the lock and was stuck in it. I had to get a locksmith to cut it out.

Bad and all as these people were, they weren't as bad as sitting tenants. I knew about these from cases my father had had in Ballina. If someone was in the house for a long time they had squatters' rights. I heard of a landlord once who put a tenant's furniture onto the street to try and get her out. She hadn't been paying the rent. She took him to court over it and won. He had to put the furniture back. It was years before he got her out. She made his life hell. That's not to say many tenants didn't suffer under cruel landlords. There were just as many of them as there were bad tenants.

As the years went on I started to do the house up more. I was lazy growing up in Ballina. It was a day's work for me to wash a cup. Now it was different. I had a goal, a selfish one. I was getting paid for it.

I converted the spare bedroom into a bathroom. That meant the tenants didn't have to go out in the cold to go to the toilet in the middle of the night. It was more stylish than our bathroom in the Villas. Everything was green. It was probably the most luxurious bathroom on the street.

Having better conditions meant I got better tenants. I learned the hard way that you had to vet them. It was almost like an interview situation. Sometimes I had to make difficult decisions.

Eventually the rent equalled the mortgage repayments. When it started to exceed it I knew I could relax. I was able to forget about the house now. Forgetting about it made me feel less like a landlord. A good year was when I didn't have to go round there at all.

Seven

I decided to join a drama group. I thought it might help me develop confidence in front of the children in the class. Didn't someone label acting the shy man's revenge?

I picked one called Delta-K. I didn't know where the name came from. Nobody else in the group seemed to know either. We were in the dark about this like we were about most other things we did when we were in it.

The director's name was Maureen. She had a thing about old stage-Irish plays. The dottier the better. I imagined her with a boxful of these curiosities up in her attic. Her ideal scenario seemed to be bucolic couples sitting in thatched cottages in the heart of the country bemoaning the vicissitudes of their fate. She'd have a shawl around her and he'd have a *dúidín*. Turfsmoke would be emanating from the chimney. She had a particular fondness for Lennox Robinson. I couldn't abide him.

We rehearsed in the basement of a pub. It was a hive of activity. Even on weekday nights there'd be a good crowd there. Seamus Heaney popped in for a drink one night. I found myself standing next to him at the counter when I came up to order a drink. We fell into conversation. I told him I'd been in UCD when he was there. It turned out he'd met Ruth on a plane once and that my name came up when they started talking. I didn't know much about him being a poet at that time. If you told me he'd win the Nobel Prize one day I'd have laughed at you. He was so laidback I almost felt like asking him if he'd like to join the group.

More drinking than acting was done in Delta-K, at least by me. I usually just got bit parts. I'd be in a scene or two and that was it. The other members of

69

the group told me I'd get bigger parts if I drank less. I told them I'd drink less if I got bigger parts. It was a vicious circle. I don't know why I drank so much. Maybe it was because we rehearsed in a pub. Maybe I was looking for some dutch courage. Maybe I was fed up of Maureen's Synge-song buffoonery.

I was never much of an actor. The contradiction of all acting is that people go into it because they like being looked at but the only way to do it well is to forget about the audience. Otherwise you're self-conscious and the process becomes transparent.

Everyone knew I wrote. That made me even more self-conscious. It was like in the school when I felt I was expected to say something profound when the subject came up. I never felt there was anything profound about being a writer. I agreed with the guy who said it was something you should do in private and then wash your hands afterwards.

Being a writer and an actor didn't work. I was mixing Apollo and Dionysius, analysis and action. I probably drank too much to get over that. It was as if I was trying to become Stan Laurel instead of Stanislavski. I was asking the group's permission to let me play the fool.

We doubled as a kind of unofficial dating agency. I later learned many drama groups have that element in them. More people were interested in hooking up with one another than studying the finer points of Greek tragedies.

I started going out with one of my co-stars. She was a pretty brunette from Mullingar. I was always more comfortable with country girls than city ones. We used to meet every Monday night. Most people hated Mondays but I didn't mind them. Anything had to be better than Sunday.

I found her very entertaining. She was full of jokes, the most corny ones you could imagine. 'Did you know Exit doors are on the way out?' 'If it wasn't for Venetian blinds it'd be curtains for all of us.' She used to go into convulsions after she told them. It was as if she was hearing them for the first time. She also did a great impersonation of Maggie Thatcher.

Sometimes I brought her to music bars. I went through a phase where I'd give my name up to sing a song or two. I didn't have much of a voice but backing was provided in these places. They could make you sound good if you got the right key. Often I didn't. Looking back now I think I sang for the same reason I acted – to get confidence in front of the public. In both activities I often pushed myself beyond my limits. I sang in a register that meant I was almost certainly going to crack on a high note when – or if – I got to it.

There was another girl in the group that I saw for a while as well, a nurse called Bridget. She was renting a house on Iona Road with two other nurses, Margaret and Breda. They were in the group as well. I used to go down to their house sometimes and stay there for hours. It was like a second home to me. Breda eventually started dating my cousin John O'Grady. He was staying with us at this time.

I introduced Margaret to a Ballina man I knew. His name was Ray Collins. He was in another drama group. He dropped in to our one now and again to see what we were at. They ended up getting married and moving to Ballina. They bought a house not too far from my Aunt Nellie's one on the Killala Road.

I was only given minor parts in the plays. 'There's no such thing as a small part,' Maureen told me, 'only a small actor.' It was a neat way out of having to offer me a decent role. These were reserved for the people who licked up to her. Or maybe they were just better actors than me.

We did dummy runs in old folks homes. A lot of the people there had dementia. They didn't notice me flubbing my lines. If I had too much to drink I got amnesia. My memory was probably worse than the eighty year olds in the audience. I felt sorry for the ones who *didn't* have dementia. They were captured audiences rather than captive ones.

I tried my best with these people. One year I got a half-decent part as a farmer in a John B. Keane play, *The Buds of Ballybunion*. I threw myself into it as much as I could. For a while I thought I was in danger of actually giving a performance. Unfortunately it didn't really materialise. Maureen pulled the curtain down on me in the middle of my big speech.

I don't think she knew what hit her. Neither did I. The curtain was hanging from a beam. The curtain and the beam fell down on me together and nearly knocked me out. Maybe that was her intention. Was she resentful of the fact that her whiskey provider was turning into an actor?

Even with the fallen curtain I continued to speak my lines. I was determined to keep going. As John B's wife put it once, 'Sometimes you just have to put on your housecoat and whore it out.' By the end of my speech I was wearing the curtain like a toga. A few of the Alzheimer people applauded. Maybe they thought I was Marc Antony from *Julius Caesar*. 'Friends, Romans, countrymen, lend me your curtains.'

We did a lot of the shows in pubs. The audiences there had less patience with my bad memory. I was usually dependent on the prompts of the cue girl. When I rolled my eyes in her direction I probably looked like Marlon Brando. He used to do that sometimes when he couldn't remember his lines and had them written on boards around the set.

I often gave my co-stars the wrong cues. That was bad enough but one time I even gave a co-star a cue from another scene. There was hell to pay about that. It reminded me of a story Peter O'Toole told about his drinking days. An interviewer asked him once if he'd ever given someone a cue from the wrong scene. 'The wrong scene?' he said, 'I gave them cues from the wrong *play*!'

Our productions never got reviewed - thankfully. The hotshot critics didn't know about us. If they got their claws into us they'd probably have written scathing accounts of our efforts at credibility. People would have come from far and wide to laugh us off the stage.

We gave free tickets to our friends and relatives. They filled the bars and tried to pretend they were enjoying themselves. Greater love than this no man hath. We forced tickets on them and pretended not to notice their horrified expressions when they came to the realisation not only that they were going to have to go out in the spills of rain to a grimy pub in the middle of nowhere to be bored out of their trees but to pay for it too. It was like the old joke, 'First prize one ticket. Second prize two tickets.'

The main pub we performed in was The Balrothery Inn. It was far enough outside the Pale to enable us to hide from the culture vultures. Our friends and relatives made the dutiful trip to Balrothery. As soon as we saw them we led them up to the bar counter. Drunk people were kinder to bad actors than sober ones. With a few jars in them we'd all become Brandos or John Gielguds. It was only the next morning as they nursed their hangovers that they'd realise how horrifically bad we were.

There was always the danger of a hard man being in the audience, someone who wasn't blinded by booze or excessive loyalty. He might even heckle. If he did, we were able for him. Example: 'This is the worst play I ever saw.' Reply: 'And you're the ugliest playgoer I ever saw. What are you going to do for a face when King Kong wants his arse back?'

Delta-K lurched on for the best part of a decade, our band of deregulated Oliviers continuing to spew bad lines from makeshift Old Vics to the woebegotten hordes who made the trek to Balrothery and then took the two sides of the road back to Dublin with them in their inebriated states.

Most of us became friends. Some of the cast offered their houses for rehearsal purposes. The acting was the boring bit. Such nights were all about the chats, the food, the drink.

Various cast members dropped in and out over the years. People like me got better parts when there was a sudden vacancy. I was always the reliable standby. It was the same in snooker and other things. I read once that Lewis Carroll said once, 'I'm a second eleven sort of guy.' I could identify with that. If I ever got to Broadway I knew I'd be the understudy.

Delta-K wasn't about whether you were good or not. It was about whether you could be at Kimmage Cross next Tuesday at five because Gary's brother had just come down with chicken pox and his Mam wasn't able to mind him.

In the last year I spent with the group we did Bernard Farrell's *All in Favour Said No.* At last we were departing from turn-of-the-century pastorals. We made a real effort with this one. Everyone went on the dry. I felt the bar we rehearsed in would have to close down due to lack of orders. Farrell even came to see it. I didn't read any reports in the following day's newspapers about him having any coronaries or seizures. Things looked good.

One of the group, a talented young man called Enda Oates, now started applying to RTE for parts. RTE? Had someone not told him we were only there for the beer? For me this was the end of the line. We were starting to become, whisper it, actors. The party was over. It was time to go so I went.

I ventured into the film world, applying for a job as an extra in a film that was being shot on the outskirts of the city. I turned up at the Burlingtown Hotel one morning at 8 a.m. Shortly afterwards a bus ferried myself and a load of other idiots to Leopardstown racecourse.

The film starred Sinead Cusack. She was beautiful. I had a crush on her. I asked her for her autograph one day. She couldn't find any paper. I had a copy of a poetry book in my pocket so she wrote it on that. I still have it.

My part was even smaller than the ones I'd been getting in Delta-K. In fact it wasn't a part at all. I had to sit in the stands in Leopardstown pretending to be looking at a horse race. There were no horses.

The film had a working title of *Steve McQueen I'm Not.* Nobody knew why. It came out as *Humboldt's Castle.* I never saw it. Someone told me it didn't get a commercial release. Why not? Had I not given a good enough performance? Maybe if I shook my head more convincingly at the horseless racecourse it might have put me in line for an Oscar.

Back in the classroom I felt I was giving a different kind of performance. At times I felt like an extra in the film of my life. I went through the motions of being a teacher but deep down I knew it wasn't me.

My attempts at becoming an actor hadn't worked. Leopardstown wasn't Clonsilla and neither was the Lincoln's Inn. I knew I was more suitable to a one-on-one situation with the pupils rather than standing in front of forty of them trying to pretend I knew what I was doing.

I made various attempts to become a remedial teacher over the next few years but that didn't work out either. If it had, I'd probably still be in the school today.

Eight

My life became taken over by my hobbies –
snooker, films, books. Music was another passion.

I loved going to The Meeting Place. It was one of
the best music bars in Dublin. A number of very
talented singers and musicians played there - Christy
Moore, Declan Sinnott, Red Peters, Don Baker,
Jimmy Faulkner. Christy Moore was the most well-
known of them but they were all brilliant in their way.
Declan Sinnott was one of the most talented guitarists
in the country. Red Peters looked like someone who
came down from the mountains when he came on
stage. I was amazed to learn he was a tax inspector by
day. The idea of it always gave me a laugh.

Don Baker was another person I used to go and
see. He played with a group called The Business in
Slattery's of Capel Street every Sunday. It was a wild
scene. People got ossified listening to him. He wore a
belt with about twenty little mouth organs on it. They
all seemed to be tuned to different keys.

Jimmy Faulkner was my favourite musician of all.
He played the jazz guitar with a group called Hotfoot.
He could almost make it talk. For my money he was
just as good as Django Reinhardt. Reinhardt was his
hero. His girlfriend told me once that he slept with his
guitar under the bed. He kept it tuned so tight that
strings sometimes snapped in the middle of the night
and woke the two of them up. It was like Bjorn Borg
with his tennis racquets.

I rarely asked members of my family to
accompany me to these sessions. Their tastes were
different. That wasn't a problem for me. We
continued to have great nights in the Villas.

Our friend Donie O'Donoghue was at many of
them. He was a great music lover too. By now he was
also an accountant and a barrister as well. He'd
probably have got on well with Red Peters, merging

the two sides of his life together, the practical and the artistic.

You never knew what to expect with Donie. If he felt like talking about a subject he'd go on about it for ages but if he didn't you couldn't get a word out of him. He used to spend ages talking to my father about weird legal cases – a man who was tried for shooting his wife because she didn't give him enough cornflakes, a man who faked his own death, a man who sued himself.

As well as going out with June, Donie also dated Jacinta. For a while I thought they were going to get married but she said he was more like a brother to her than anything else.

He arrived at the house at all hours of the day and night. He'd often be sitting at the kitchen table with the paper sprawled across it when I came home from work. There'd hardly be room to eat. He'd get engrossed in some article and hardly notice you were there or bother talking to you. Sometimes I felt as if I was in his house rather than him being in ours.

One night he came round to the Villas with three Kris Kristofferson LPs. All I knew about Kristofferson at that time was the song 'Sunday Mornin' Comin' Down. I used to sing it sometimes at parties. Donie made it his business to educate me more about him. He played the records over and over until dawn, telling me everything about his life as we listened to them.

From knowing practically nothing about Kristofferson I became something of an authority on him thanks to Donie. He didn't think of asking me if I wanted to go to bed that night. Bed was only for boring people. In fact he never thought of asking me if I might want to do anything at all other than listen to his records until the sun came up. He'd seen Keith and other members of the family staying up all night on previous occasions. They'd discuss films and have tea and burnt toast at dawn as the birds began their dawn chorus. He knew we were night owls.

After breakfast he said he had to go somewhere. He was always disappearing on these mysterious missions. Then he'd come back just as suddenly with some other fixation.

There were never enough hours in the day for him. I remember being over in his flat in Frankfurt Avenue in Rathgar one night. It was well after midnight. I was getting ready to go home. I asked him if he'd ring a taxi for me. 'I'll do better than that,' he said, 'I'll drive you into town. I'm going to go to a dance.' He always made decisions on the spur of the moment. One night he even jumped on a plane for America because he was thirsty and the pub he was in was closing. He didn't think about the fact that he'd have to come back. That kind of stuff was for boring people too.

I joined a snooker league. I'd never liked my name so I started calling myself Peter. Having been born on Saint Patrick's Day I always wondered why my father didn't call me Pat - or Paddy like his nephew.

The full name on my birth certificate was Aubrey de Vere Patrick Dillon-Malone. It was a bit of a mouthful. I always wished I was called something more simple like John Murphy. Being saddled with it gave me a love for more digestible names. Maybe we all love our opposites. Engelbert Humperdinck was born George Dorsey. If I was born Engelbert Humperdinck I think I'd have changed it to something like George Dorsey. It came as a shock to me to learn that you can't legally change your Christian name, only your surname. I'd dropped the Dillon many years ago. I only used it when I wanted to sound posh. If I was writing to *The Guardian* or *The Telegraph* it got people's attention.

I first started using Peter when I joined a chess club in the Lincoln's Inn in the eighties. I spotted an ad for it one night before a Delta-K rehearsal. The club was next door to the pub. There were about a dozen of us in it. We used to be ferried around in a coach to take on other teams in places like Skerries and Malahide. That phase of my life is hazy now. It's hard to believe I took it so seriously. I started buying books on things like the Grumfeld Attack and the Hodgson Defence. For a while I thought I might take the game up professionally. I got a rude awakening when I started getting beaten by people half my age. One night in Skerries this little whippersnapper played five of us at the one time and won all five games. He looked about twelve. That was the night I got cured of chess as a possible career. He was so cocky he took away all my love of the game. I felt like stuffing the bishop down his throat.

I stuck to the name Peter after retiring from professional chess. I got so fond of it I eventually started to believe it was my real name. If someone called it out on the street I'd turn around. I remember seeing a film once called *The Stepfather*. It was about this guy who kept changing his name and marrying different women. He was in search of the ideal marriage. None of his wives satisfied him so he started killing them. There was one scene that struck a chord with me. It had him getting a phone call and looking confused. He looked into the middle distance and went, 'Who am I here?' He's had so many identities he can't remember his latest one.

My snooker wasn't any better as Peter than it was when I was going by my own name. My ambition was to be a bad good player but I didn't quite get that far. All I became was a good bad player.

Playing in the league matches adrenalized me. I liked competition even when I lost. Much better players than me preferred playing for fun. That never did anything for me. There had to be something at stake even if it was only a fiver. I turned up for the

Christmas competition every year. The prize was a turkey. The entry fee cost more than it.

I felt I was a liability to the team. In the fliers I usually got a head start on the better players. I'd often get ten or twenty points up on them. I was good at holding on to these points against fluent potters. I'd make the table awkward to stop them getting into a rhythm. They hated me for that. Some of them even refused to play me. One fellow said, 'You're so negative you should be sponsored by Kodak.' some of them were very witty.

I didn't have the advantage of the extra points in the league matches. It had to be a level playing field there. Everyone started at zero. Sometimes I got slaughtered. The other guy would often be over fifty before I potted my first ball.

'Why don't you concentrate more on what you're good at?' my mother said to me one day.

Doing what I was good at bored me more often than not. It was too easy. Jimmy White once said he wanted to be remembered as someone who played snooker the hard way. I liked that quote. If he played it differently he'd probably have won a rake of world titles but what good would that have been to him?

I didn't know much about Jimmy at this point of my life. He'd been at Sheffield once before but got squeezed out 10-8 by Steve Davis in the first round. This year he was playing my hero Alex Higgins.

I'd followed Higgins' career from when he beat John Spencer to lift the world crown as a nobody in 1972. Spencer didn't know what hit him when 'Hurricane' Higgins arrived. His life off the table was just as compelling as his one on it. Often he wasn't just on the back pages of the newspapers but the front as well – and maybe the middle. He had an addiction to drink and gambling as well as snooker. Barry Hearn said, 'I don't think he ever won a bet in his life.' Jimmy White said he was the worst loser he ever saw. One time he tried to throw a television out of a window in anger after backing a loser but it was a reinforced one. It bounced back at him, knocking him onto a sofa. If it wasn't so tragic it might have been funny.

Higgins saved snooker from its anodyne qualities, replacing the bow tie with the leather jacket, the clean fingernail guys with the whiff of cordite. I went to Goff's sales ring one night. That was where the Benson & Hedges Irish Masters was staged. It was so big it was like a gladiatorial arena. I saw him beat Cliff Thorburn 5-4 after coming back from 4-nil. I got so excited I ran out into the car park and told everyone they weren't allowed to drive home. A car ran over my foot. I was drinking so much I didn't feel the pain till the next morning.

Jimmy was like his spiritual godson. He looked quieter but he was capable of raising hell in his own way. On the table he did everything Higgins did and more. The difference between them, someone said, was that Higgins did the impossible and made a show of it. Jimmy did it almost laconically.

They faced one another in the world championship semi-final in Sheffield that year. It was up to 16. Jimmy went into a 15-14 lead. He was 59 points to nil up in the 30th frame. He only needed a few more points to win but Higgins pulled off a remarkable break to tie the match. Jimmy was, as they say, 'gone' and lost the decider. The defeat defined the future pattern of his career. He never won a world title despite six appearances in finals.

1982 was the year of upsets. Higgins was regarded as a has-been by many coming up to the world final. Davis was expected to win it but he fell victim to the first round curse, being dumped out 10-2 by Tony Knowles at that stage.

Jimmy Connors won Wimbledon that year. Like Higgins he was another blast from the past. The only time he won it before that was in 1974. John McEnroe was expected to devour him.

The shocks didn't end there. Northern Ireland beat Spain in a World Cup qualifier after Gerry Armstrong scored a goal in the 47th minute. When I saw they were 7/1 to win I put a bet on them. I don't know why. We obviously weren't in Spain's class. Maybe I felt the odds were too good to resist in a two-horse race even if it was a David and Goliath affair. I made a pretty penny on that bet.

Offaly beat Kerry in the all-Ireland a few months later. Kerry were going for the five-in-a-row. They looked set to achieve that when they went two points up as full time approached. Seamus Derby scored a freak goal in the dying seconds to deny them.

Jimmy played hard to get with me. He'd always reminded me of the Artful Dodger on the snooker table, running away with frames while you'd be looking around you. In real life he did the same to me. I tried to meet him many times over the next few years. Finally I succeeded. It was on a Monday morning. The previous day he'd been beaten in the final of the Irish tournament at Goffs sales ring in Naas.

He was dressed in a tracksuit, a contrast from his more usual tuxedos. He had his legs crossed on a sofa. The expression on his face said, 'Over to you.' It felt good to me to be having a pint of Smithwicks with my hero at eleven o'clock in the morning in a luxurious emporium.

I didn't get much out of him. Only in later years would I learn about his wild life, about him freebasing drugs with Kirk Stevens in the Shelbourne, about him taking his dead brother's body from a mortuary and bringing it home to wake him in the family home. All he gave me were monosyllables no matter how many questions I asked him.

'He does his talking with his hands,' Hugo said to me. He was right. I heard he had them insured for £1 million.

Alex Higgins had more to say. He talked about the wild escapades, the bans, the stabbings, the falling out of windows, the peeing into potted plants. I'd met him a few times over the years at Goff's. He rattled on about this and that. At a certain point, you were always afraid he'd go off on one.

I also talked to Steve Davis. He was as engaging off the table as he was annoying on it. His wit meant nothing to me. He'd bored me for too many years with his style of play. It was no good being Mr Nice Guy (or even Mr Entertaining Guy) off the table. He was the Maggie Thatcher of the green baize.

Over the next few months I started making phone calls to Jimmy at different venues. I used to give him advice about his game. I'd ring him at all hours of the day and night. I told him I wasn't just a fan but a writer as well – a fan with a typewriter. That seemed to give me more of a standing with him.

I'd say things like 'You shouldn't have gone into the pack against Warren King.' King was a mediocre player who beat him 5-2 in an inconsequential tournament. It was at a time when everyone seemed to be able to beat him if they got him with a hangover or on a day when he didn't seem to care. That was a lot of the time.

One day after a ridiculous defeat I rang him up and said, 'Maybe you should have put more screw on the cue ball when you were on the green in the second frame.' He was like, 'What?'

He always took the calls but he never commented on what I was saying. All I usually got was 'Cheers, mate, nice to hear from you,' in that gravelly voice. I must have seemed like a stalker to him. Maybe he even thought I was gay.

Anytime he lost I felt a national day of mourning should be announced. If it was in an early round of a tournament I felt the whole thing should have been cancelled. Who could be interested in watching the other players in it?

A record 18.5 million people watched Dennis Taylor beat Davis in the 1985 final. It went down to the last ball. I always enjoyed seeing Davis being beaten but the match itself wasn't very high quality. People forgot that. For most of the time it was about drama, not excellence.

As Jimmy's losing run continued in the following years I started to bet against him. It was like an insurance policy. The improvement in my financial position prevented me putting my head in the oven. I usually got good odds against him losing even if he was in terrible form. Bookies never seemed to take account of that. Or maybe they kept the odds low because so many people were betting on him to win. The tic-tac man John McCririck said, 'If Jimmy was a race horse, bookies would keep him in free oats for the rest of his life.' Bookies often said to me, 'You must really hate that guy.' Little did they know. Every time he lost I went into a deep gloom. The money I won helped alleviate it a bit.

If I bet against him, I told myself, he'd win. And vice versa. He got to a world final in 1984 but lost to Steve Davis. He was 12-4 down after the first day's play. He came back to 17-16 the next day but eventually lost 18-16. Brilliant comebacks that didn't result in victories became a hallmark of his game over the next decade or so.

Davis was his main nemesis. I got to hate him for the defeats he inflicted on him until I learned to accept the fact that if it wasn't him it would have been someone else. The problem was Jimmy. As my mother used to say, 'There's one born every minute and two to take him.'

Whenever a tournament wasn't on the television I used to ring the newspapers up for updates on the scores. I didn't have teletext so it was my only recourse. *The Irish Times* was the main place I rang. It helped if he was playing an Irish player, someone like Taylor.

'Can you give me the score on the Taylor match?' I'd say.

I never mentioned Jimmy's name. They'd think it was unpatriotic that I'd be more interested in a cockney than a fellow countryman. After Taylor retired I used to run into the same situation with players like Ken Doherty if he was playing Jimmy. I'd say, 'Can you give me the score on the Doherty match?'

It was always Jimmy I was looking for. I was desperate for him to win but his career was littered with senseless defeats. A lot of thee were caused by his brittle temperament. Clive James said he reminded him of a fighter pilot on amphetamines.

If I couldn't get to his matches and they weren't being televised, I used to 'watch' them on teletext. Sometimes I felt I could affect the outcome by mental energy. I thought it would give him good karma. If it was a best-of-nine match and it went to 4-4 I'd look at the 4 beside his name and try to get it to change into a 5. It didn't always happen but it did sometimes, That was good enough for me. The Gods were smiling down on us.

I brought my mother out to see him in a match at Goffs in 1983. He lost to Dennis Taylor. It was a bad match, so bad I couldn't even watch it. Taylor meant nothing to me even though he was Irish. As he closed in on victory I had to leave the auditorium. My mother was distraught. She said, 'Why do you drive me out all this way and you won't even watch the match?' I couldn't explain it. I took it too seriously. She liked the little boy lost in Jimmy but she could never get worked up about him the way I did. It was a day out for her, a day spoiled by my bad manners. She'd done herself up to the nines for it and now that was all wasted. I'd ruined it for her just like Jimmy ruined it for me.

She died in 1985. I found her death much harder to take than that of my father. She had cancer and was in a lot of pain. Why hadn't she died quickly like him? How could God be so cruel? Theology could explain it by saying 'Whom the lord loveth, he chastiseth.' That meant nothing to me. Neither did it mean anything to say she was taken from us so she could pray for us in heaven. I looked on slogans like that the same way I looked at the bromides you got in fortune cookies or Christmas crackers.

The year after her death I got married to Mary, the girl who met Irving Layton in Aran. She was from Galway. She reminded me of my mother in many ways. They both had the same quietness, the same depth. Both of us had roots in Roscommon. That gave us an extra connection. Connacht people are tribal. We recognise something in one another that nobody else can see. It's endemic, like a secret code.

I got to know Galway as well as Mary got to know Ballina over the years. We went on visits to both places, sharing anecdotes about our youth as we walked streets that were so familiar to each of us. Both of us had been uprooted from the west to go to Dublin in our teenage years. We shared these stories too. Galway and Mayo became like two sides of the same coin from that point of view. They became equally familiar to us with the recycling of such anecdotes.

Nine

One year during the summer holidays I decided to go down to Ballina and have it out with Creeper. Sometimes I thought I might have exaggerated what he did to me in my mind. I'd read stories of people who did that, convincing themselves things were worse than they were because they were so far in the past. It was like how everything seemed bigger when you were young, buildings and people and places. If you re-visited them as an adult you realised how mistaken you were.

Mary encouraged me to go. She thought I needed closure on him if I was to move on with my life. She knew I was worrying the wound. She thought I'd missed an opportunity the last time I was in Ballina with my father. Now I had another one. I had to grab it, to free myself from the control he was still exerting on my mind.

We stayed in the Downhill Inn outside the town. For the first few days of our trip we did the things most visitors to the town did. We went around the shops and walked the beach at Enniscrone. At night we had a few jars.

One night we fell into conversation with a man of my own vintage. As the bar was about to close I mentioned the dreaded subject of Creeper. His eyes grew wide as I went into the details. He was a year ahead of me and didn't have him for any subjects.

'I knew he was tough,' he said, 'but not that tough.'

I said I didn't know if he was alive or dead.

'He retired,' he said, 'I think he got a parish in Lahardaun.'

I greeted this information as if it was some casual piece of news but my heart started to thump as I took it in. I felt as if I was a private detective who'd just got a key piece of information about a criminal.

When I thought about it, where else would he have been but Lahardaun? He never stopped talking about the place.

After the pub closed we walked back to the Inn. I was in a state of confusion. For years I'd thought about this moment. Now that it was here I was apprehensive about it. Maybe it'd bring back the old scars more than ever.

I asked Mary what she thought I should do.

'You'll never forgive yourself if you don't see him,' she said, 'Especially now that you know where he lives.' I knew she was right.

We checked out of the Inn soon afterwards. Later that evening we drove out to where he lived. My stomach churned for the whole journey. It was almost as bad as the way it was when I cycled across the bridge to Muredach's every morning for the four years I was taught by him.

After asking a few people for directions we got to where his house easily enough. It was on the banks of Lough Conn. I knew that would have been heaven to him. It was somewhere he could fish all day now that he had no more parish duties to perform.

His house looked like something out of a cowboy film. It was a bungalow with smoke billowing out of the chimney. Nephin stood behind it like a benign presence.

I parked across the road. Mary looked at me expectantly. I found myself breathing heavily as I tried to figure out what to do. I wasn't sure what I was going to find. Would I hit him? Would some beast come out of me that I didn't know existed as I sought to gain revenge for what he put me through?

'What's keeping you?' she said as I sat there, 'Why aren't you going over to him?'

'I'm wondering if it's a good idea. I don't know if I'm ready.'

'If I hear that again I'll scream. If you're not ready now you'll never be.'

I couldn't get out of the car. It was as if I was still the child of long ago. I couldn't face him.

It was getting on to evening. I kept looking across at his house, at the field behind it where some cows were grazing. The longer I waited, I knew, the harder it would be to move. She had to give me a push in the end.

I got out.

'Good luck,' she said, 'Have you got your bullet-proof vest on you?'

'It's him that'll be needing that.'

'If I hear any shots I'll come in after you.'

I walked across the street with my chest heaving. I stood outside the door for a few minutes and then I knocked. I could hear movement inside. Footsteps slow came towards the door.

It opened. A face I didn't recognise looked quizzically at me. He was in his soutane. His hair was totally grey, or at least what remained of it. His hands were shaking. For a moment I thought he might have been afraid of me. But of course that was ridiculous. There was no way he could have known who I was. Too many years had elapsed.

He was dressed in a crumpled black suit. There was something cooking in the kitchen behind him.

'What can I do for you?' he said in a thin voice.

I asked him if I could come in. He looked confused.

'Of course,' he said.

I walked inside.

'You haven't broken down or anything, have you?' he said, 'I saw a car across the street.'

'No. It's fine.'

He motioned me to a chair. There was another one opposite it that he sat into. Beside it was a Bible. It had a bookmark in it as if he'd just been reading.

Everything in the room looked spartan – the floor, the walls, the furniture. You'd easily have known it was a priest's house. There was an electric globe on a table in the corner. I recognised it from Muredach's. He used to plug it in to show us all the countries of the world for his geography class. It lit up like a pumpkin when he did that. Outside the window the gentle slopes of Nephin glided towards the sea.

He looked at me with a strained expression.

'I'm an old pupil of yours,' I said.

'Ah.' He relaxed into his chair.

'What's your name?' he said. I told him. He remembered me immediately.

'I taught your brothers,' he said, 'They were lovely lads. Didn't Clive become a Jesuit?'

I told him he did.

'And Keith, and Hugo and Basil.'

'You have a good memory.'

'Didn't you all leave at the end of the sixties?'

'Yes. In 1969. My father retired.'

'How is he?'

'He died.'

'I'm sorry to hear that. What about the rest of you?'

'Keith is an accountant. Hugo went in for teaching. Basil is an engineer in America.'

'I knew you'd all do well.'

He started talking about his own family.

'Did you know my nephew is playing for Mayo?'

'I do.'

I used to see him on the television every now and then. He was a talented player but I couldn't watch him. It was like referred blame. I didn't want him to be good.

'Hopefully he'll help Mayo land the big one sometime soon.'

'Hopefully.'

The county had reached a few All-Irelands in the past few years but failed to win any.

'What do you think of the curse?' he said.

He was referring to a spell there was said to have been put on the team by a priest in 1951. That was the last year they'd won. The priest thought they hadn't shown respect for a funeral on their way home from Croke Park. Apparently the coach they were travelling in hadn't slowed down when the cortege passed them.

'There are only a few of that team still alive,' I said.

'Just one, I believe.'

'Maybe we should shoot him.'

He smiled.

'Do you still shout for Mayo when they're playing Dublin?'' he said.

'Louder than ever.'

'Good on you.'

'Even if I spent a hundred years in Dublin I could never become a Dubliner.'

We talked about trivial things – changes in the town, the Celtic Tiger, the slow pace of his life since he retired. He asked me if I'd like a cup of tea. I said I would. As he went to put on the kettle his hands shook so much I wasn't sure if he was going to be able to make it to the cooker or not. I offered to help but he waved me away.

'It's the old Parkinson's,' he laughed.

I got a shock when he said that. I couldn't believe someone could be casual about something so serious.

I asked him how long he'd had it.

'Nearly three years now,' he said. 'It's a nuisance but they have great pills for it now. They slow it down. I suppose you have to have something at my age.' He gave a rueful smile.

The kettle boiled. He poured the water into two cups. The saucer shook as he came over to me with my one.

I felt guilty. His illness had scuppered my plan. He was too weak to wreak revenge on. Maybe, I should just finish the tea and say nothing to him. How could I give out to an old man who had Parkinson's disease? He didn't seem to remember me as being any different from anyone else in his class that year. If I walked out now the hatchet would be buried. Could I do that?

I didn't know. A part of me knew I'd never be at ease if I didn't have it out with him. I needed to do that even if nothing came of it. I needed to do it because of the amount of time I spent thinking about him since I left Ballina.

He nibbled at a biscuit. I stood up.

'You made my childhood miserable,' I said.

He frowned.

'I beg your pardon?' he said.

He put the biscuit down.

'I did what?'

'You terrorised me when I was in your class.'

He didn't seem to know what I was talking about. He smiled. It was the same smile as of old, the first connection to my past. As it spread across his face he was the tyrant again, a man delighting in the bestowing of pain.

I tapped his shoulder with my fist.

'Do you remember that?' I said.

He shook his head amusedly.

'I don't know what you're getting at,' he said, 'Did I hit you when you were a boy?'

I wasn't sure if he genuinely forgot or if he was playing a game with me.

'You once used my shoulder for target practice.'

He seemed to be confused. I didn't know whether to pursue the subject or not. We sat in the silence.

Suddenly I felt foolish. Was I making a mountain out of a molehill? Was the past a figment of my imagination? Had I exaggerated it wildly in my mind? Maybe he was no worse than any of them. I thought of a film I'd seen as a child called *The Day of the Triffids.* It struck terror into me at the time but when I saw it years later it was more like a comedy. Maybe Creeper was like that too. A comic illusion.

'Was I rough?' he said. 'You may be right. I'm uncertain. You have the advantage of me.'

As I looked at him I thought: Could this really be the man I once feared? He looked old suddenly, old and frail. Maybe he was as much a victim of life as I was.

He couldn't have much to look forward to in his condition. I remembered another film I'd seen, a more famous one than *The Day of the Triffids.* It was one called *Judgment At Nuremburg.* It was about the trial of Nazi war criminals. Burt Lancaster played one of them. He was given a big speech towards the end. One of the lines in it was used to describe one of the criminals. It described him as 'an old man crying into his Bible.' Creeper was that man for me now.

'Whatever I did to you,' he said, 'I'm sorry.'

He winced in pain. When he took his cup up he started to shake. He quivered so much he wasn't able to drink from it. It started to spill onto the floor.

I took it from him.

'Thank you,' he said, 'I'm embarrassed.'

He asked me to tell him more about my brothers. I didn't want to but something about his eyes made me. They were pleading.

It felt strange talking to him about them. I hadn't even known he taught them. I never mentioned him to them for fear I'd say too much.

He looked lost in his memories.

'Didn't your father come down here for a court case a few years ago?' he said then.

'He did.'

'Were you with him?'

'Yes.'

'And your mother?'

'No. She didn't come with us.'

'She's a lovely woman,' he said.

Whenever anyone talked to me about her over the years it was always with a sense of reverence. Mentions of my father were usually followed by smiles or maybe an anecdote. Something he said in the court maybe, a quotable comment to a judge or a clever riposte in a pub. He was a creature of the earth, like them. My mother, in contrast, resided on some more ethereal plateau. This was apparent to everyone. All you had to do was mention her name and they'd go, 'Ah.'

'And yourself,' he said then, 'What about you. I suppose you're in some job or other.'

'I became a teacher,' I said. I watched his face for a reaction but there was none. He just nodded.

'How do you find the children in Dublin?' he said, 'I believe some of them can be very bold.'

'That they are.'

'I'm sure they're a lot different to when you were their age.'

For a second I thought he was playing with me again, trying to prise something out of me.

'If you give them an inch they'll take a mile.'

He chuckled.

'Maybe it was always the way,' he said, 'though I never had any trouble with the Dillon-Malones.'

No, I thought to myself, but the Dillon-Malones had trouble with you. At least this one did.

I wasn't sure where to go from there. Would I let him off the hook or rub his nose in what he did?

I listened to the ticking of a clock, the lowing of cattle outside. How ordinary his life was now, how peaceful. Was I going to disturb that? Would it be worth it for some petty vengeance? His confusion, whether real or feigned, made me feel cruel, even ridiculous. And yet I couldn't leave the house without getting something out of him, some detail that might solve the puzzle for me.

'Did you have a problem with me because I was a solicitor's son?' I said, 'Were you resentful of that?'

He looked at me as if he was seeing me for the first time. Then he reached into his soutane. I thought of the way he used to reach into it for his cane. All he took out now was a pair of rosary beads. He lay them on his lap.

'There's something I have to tell you,' he said. 'I never wanted to be a teacher. I dreaded the idea of spending my life in Muredach's. My dream was to go on the Missions. I had my heart set on Nigeria. I read everything I could get my hands on about it.'

The lines disappeared from his face as he spoke. He became like a young man again, a man for whom the world was an ocean of possibilities.

He frowned.

'Unfortunately it didn't work out like that,' he said.

I asked him what happened.

'The bishop wouldn't let me go. There was a shortage of priests in Muredach's at the time. They put me into teacher training college instead. I was shoved into a job I wasn't suited for. If I was tough with you maybe it was because I was afraid of losing control of the class. I never had confidence in myself. Maybe I swung the lead so nobody would suspect that.'

For a moment he wasn't Creeper. He was another person.

I asked him what his childhood was like. He took a deep breath as his past came back to him.

'We never had much money,' he said. 'I was the first member of my family to go to secondary school.

Everyone was proud of me. Big things were expected. I'll never forget the day of my ordination. Everyone came from the surrounding parishes as I got back to Lahardaun. There was bunting all over the street I lived on. They even had a band playing. You'd think I'd been made Pope. I was looking forward to telling my mother I was going to go to Nigeria. Then the bishop called me up to his palace to talk to me. He told me he didn't want me to go on the Missions. It hit me like a bombshell. He wouldn't listen to me telling him how much I had my heart set on it.'

'Why not?'

'I don't know. If I was from a well-off family he might have. The thinking then was that poor people went into seminaries for no better reason than to get an education. After they were ordained you could do what you liked with them. My mother died the following year. It was the worst time of my life. Suddenly I didn't care what I did. I gave in.'

The years ebbed away as he talked. I was back in Muredach's and he was standing in front of me, wedged between the two desks. Except now I was seeing him as he was now. He wasn't to be feared anymore, just pitied.

I found a tear in my eye, whether for myself or him I didn't know. He looked like a child - a helpless, hopeless child. I wanted to reassure him, to tell him everything was fine, that I forgave him - if there was anything to forgive.

How many more were like him, I wondered. How many people were dumped into seminaries against their will? Were we all where we were because of circumstances rather than our own wishes and desires?

He started to breathe deeply. It was as if he was about to cry. I wanted to go over to him but I couldn't bring myself to do that. I thought to myself: I could have made this call thirty years ago and saved myself three decades of hand-wringing. How many other agonies were the result of bad memories?

'I'm sorry if I upset you,' I said but he didn't seem to hear me.

'I was wet behind the ears when I entered the priesthood,' he said, 'My father had just died. I was in a kind of trauma. Maybe I wanted to run away from life. Maybe my vocation was an escape for me, not a real vocation.'

He recalled his early years in the seminary, how he felt out of place with people more clued into life than he was.

'All I could talk about was fishing,' he said, 'fishing and farming. The other lads had more life knowledge than me. They were more widely read. I was embarrassed in their company. For the first few months I wanted to go home. I kept ringing my parents. I cried into the phone some nights. But I stuck it out. That's the thing about life. You have to stick it out.'

'Why didn't you tell the bishop you had your heart set on Nigeria?'

'It wouldn't have done any good. He didn't like people not taking his word as law. He might have sent me to a bad parish if I stood up to him. After a while I stopped caring. Then it was back to the books, the books I hated.'

The more he talked the more I felt ashamed of myself. I was ashamed of the fact that I was so locked into my world I forgot about the fact that other people had problems. He'd been like a monolith to me. how could I have known he was like jelly inside how many more were there like him ? It didn't matter that they had power, that they were bigger than you, older than you.

Had he been right to see me as someone privileged? Someone who had notions about themselves as the son of a solicitor in a small town?

Was he right to try and pull me down from what he saw as my high horse even if I didn't know I was on one?

'Did it ever get any easier for you?' I asked him.

'To be fair it did. I got to accept it in time. The holidays were good. I spent a month or two on Lough Conn every summer. That's where I was happiest, fishing and not having to think.'

'What about your life in Muredach's? How did that go?'

'I taught some fine boys. Some of them went on to university like yourself. I always liked it when that happened.'

I was surprised to hear him saying he liked people going to university. Had I even got him wrong about that?

'My prayer life has been very fulfilling to me too. You don't have to be in Nigeria to pray. In the last few year, unfortunately, I haven't even been able to get out to the church much.'

'Is that because of the Parkinson's?'

'I had some problems with my heart. They led to early retirement. It was a precaution more than anything else. The doctor said I'd be giving myself the best chance of a long life if I slowed down. Then the Parkinson's hit me.'

'It must be tough for you.'

'It's not too bad. You get used to it.'

'Are you able to cater for yourself?'

'A girl comes in every day. Annie. She's my lifesaver. We have some good chats. She keeps me up to date with what's going on in the world.'

'What about your family? Do you have brothers and sisters?'

'Two of each. They're scattered all over the country. They drop in on me when they can but it isn't always easy for them to get off work. It would be

98

nice to visit them but I'm afraid those days are gone now.'

'Do you go out at all?'

'No. I'd be afraid of falling.'

'It must be hard for you to fill the days.'

'I watch television a good bit. It's mostly rubbish but it passes the time. I love it when the football season starts.'

His hands started shaking again. He clasped them in one another to stop them.

He looked at his watch.

'Is it that time already?' he said, 'I mustn't talk anymore. It tires me and I'm sure it bores you. I don't know what came over me telling you all these things about myself.'

'I'm glad you did.'

I looked out the window. It was getting dark. I didn't know what to do. Was I guilty or was there still some anger there? He'd changed from the fiery young priest he was to a mellow old man. Could I make that transition too?

He stood up.

'Would you like another cup of tea?' he said.

'No thanks. I should be going now. I've taken up enough of your time.'

He went over to the sink. He rinsed the cups under it.

'Did I see someone else in your car?' he said.

'That's my wife.'

'You didn't tell me you were married.'

'We never got around to that.'

'She must be freezing out there. Would you not ask her to come in?'

'We have to be back in Dublin. I've already stayed much longer than I intended.'

'That's a pity. I hope you'll call again now that you've broken the ice. If you do, bring her in with you. I'd like to meet her.'

'I will.'

'It's nice to see people. Life can get lonely here. I promise not to talk about myself if you call back.'

'Don't say that. It was interesting listening to you.'

'Now you're just being polite.'

I told him I'd drop in on him the next time I was down but I knew I wouldn't. There would have been no point. Even if I didn't blame him for anything he did I could never have a relationship with him. Too much had happened to prevent that.

I stood up. Even though he was stooped with the Parkinson's he still towered over me. I said goodbye to him. He gave me as firm a handshake as he could. As I went towards the door I thought he looked lost.

'You were good to come and see me,' he said, 'Not many people do. Maybe I made too many enemies in the classroom.'

'I don't think so. People speak very highly of you.' I wasn't sure if they did or not because I never talked to people about him. I just wanted to say it. Maybe if I said it enough I'd believe it. I wanted to believe it even if it was a lie.

'Give my best to your family,' he said at the door.

'I will.'

'Once again I'm sorry if I ever did anything to hurt you. We do things in life without realising who we're upsetting.'

'I probably had too thin a skin. If I did, you did me a favour by thickening it.'

'I wouldn't have wanted to be the person responsible for that. Life does it anyway.'

I shook his hand again.

'Thanks for straightening me out,' I said.

There was nothing more to say. I moved to go. I thought I saw a sad smile on his lips as he closed the door.

I stood for a few moments on the doorstep listening to his steps shuffling away. Then it was quiet. For a moment I felt like going back in. If I did, though, what would I have said? That a monkey been taken off my back? That I came to him for one thing and got another?

I walked back to the car. A part of me felt cleansed and a part flat. Maybe, I thought, we treasure our grievances so much we miss them when they go away. Or when they're taken from us. Was I a liar to have made a monster out of him? Was it all much ado about nothing?

Mary was standing outside the car when I got back to it.

'I thought you were going to stay the night,' she said, 'What happened?'

'To be honest with you I'm not sure.'

'Well at least you didn't come to blows.'

When I didn't say anything she said, 'Or did you?'

I found myself laughing. She laughed too.

'He's not the worst,' I said, 'We sorted out a few things.'

'What sorts of things?'

'I don't want to talk about it yet. For the moment I just want to relax. I feel a bit strange.'

The years of brooding on him had taken their toll. I had no resilience left. I needed to forget about him now, to forget everything that happened so I could make way for new things in my life, things I'd stopped myself experiencing because of him, things of an adult.

'Is that all I get after an hour waiting?' she said.

'Give me time to let it sink in. Then I'll tell you everything.'

I gunned the engine.

'Do you still hate him?' she said, 'At least tell me that much.'

'No. It's all gone now.'

'He looked like a nice man from what I could see of him. Has the old devil reformed?'

'Maybe. Or maybe I have.'

We'd intended to stay somewhere in the midlands that night but I was too worked up to stop the car and look for a place. I told her I wanted to drive straight to Dublin if she didn't mind. She said that was fine.

She wanted to hear the details of the conversation but I couldn't tell them to her. In many ways I felt embarrassed about the whole thing. Maybe she'd have thought I was a fraud if I went into any detail about it.

I drove all the way to Dublin like a madman. When I got to the house I went straight to bed. She was dying of curiosity but I couldn't satisfy it, not that day or the next or the one after that. The longer the time went by I felt there was no need to say anything. She stopped asking me and we got on with other things. I felt I'd got him out of my system. I wanted to forget him.

Ten

Life in Dublin went on as usual. I found myself watching more Gaelic football than I used to. After a while it grew on me. I watched Creeper's nephew when he put on the Mayo jersey. It was like a weight being lifted from me to be able to appreciate his skills.

Mayo played well with his help. I realised that I enjoyed the game just as much as soccer once I gave myself over to it. Maybe I didn't inherit my father's pro-British tendencies after all. Maybe what I hadn't liked about football growing up was the sense of defeat it seemed to always bring with it rather than the game itself. Muredach's lost more games than they won but Mayo were different. They had real talent even if they couldn't scale that final hurdle and win an All-Ireland.

I still had dreams about Creeper. They were always the same. It was a cold morning. He was standing at the desk punching me. I was cowering under his tall frame, his soutane. A smile was still playing about his lips. He was lodged in my mind like something I couldn't remove, a film clip re-wound through the spools of memory.

I found my concentration drifting at work. When that happened the children copped it. They were still doing their psychology on me, working out how far they could go before I'd snap. Sometimes making me snap became a kind of game to them.

I did my best to teach them but sometimes I felt I was irrelevant. What did it matter whether I taught them or someone else did? They'd graduate anyway, or fail to. There were probably only about two or three people in any given class you could mould. The others were going to do what they did regardless of your influence. Maybe it was true what people said – primary teachers were only glorified babysitters.

In the evenings I continued to play poor snooker in the leagues. We travelled all over Dublin for our games. Not all of the venues were salubrious. I played against sharks with beer bellies in grimy pubs and clubs. A lot of them were drinkers. With a pint in your hand you felt you could do the impossible. Just like big drinkers think they're good drivers, they also think they're great snooker players – until they miss a sitter. Or hit a bollard.

The worse I played the more I believed in myself. Some nights I felt I couldn't miss if I tried. I was God.Once in a blue moon I even won a match.

The drink steadied me. It made me brave. I wasn't walking a greased tightrope with it. It fired me up with a crazy kind of enthusiasm, blotting out all the mistakes of the past.

I was the only one on the team with a car so I ferried everyone to the away venues. Some of them joked that it was the only reason I was kept on. Every year our club seemed to prop up the end of the table. One year we won but I wasn't playing. I had the flu. Maybe that's why we won. I got a subs trophy as a consolation prize. It has a statue of a snooker player on it. I still have it. When people admire it I don't go into the details of how I got it. The fact is that I was lying in bed sick when we won. I had to face the fact that I was more use to the team as a patient than as a player. The greatest favour I ever did them was not turning up.

One of the young whizzkids took my place and gobbled up the opposition. He was hardly out of short pants. At that age nobody knew what fear was. They hadn't experienced defeat so they laughed at the threat of it. Their bravado made their opponents nervous. It was a vicious circle.

The trophy that was presented to us probably meant more to me than to the people who actually played to win it. They were good at the game so they took success for granted. I never won anything before that so it became precious to me. I gave it pride of place in the attic. At least there it was out of harm's way. I didn't display it anywhere else. I had at least that much integrity. I liked looking at it, at the gilt player bent over the table, his frame like the frame of a cue itself. It probably should have been a statue of a car instead of a snooker player. That was my main contribution to the team – my four wheels.

Putting so much effort into my snooker ate into my commitment to teaching. I was also writing a lot now. That took time too, time I should probably have used to correct copies.

One day I got a phone call from an NUJ man telling me I was writing too much for a teacher, that I was taking work away from fulltime journalists. He was Dutch. 'You vill haf to join ze union, he said, 'Eet ees necessary vor you to make up your mind which job eet ees you vant to do.'

When I applied for membership of the NUJ I was informed I couldn't be admitted unless I proved that I was earning two-thirds of my income from journalism. But how could I be doing that? It was one of those chicken and egg situations. You couldn't be a member unless you wrote and you couldn't write unless you were a member. I had to crunch the numbers to get in.

At the time I was earning about a tenth of my income from writing. Writers usually ask for their earnings to be undercut on accounts statements. I was in the unusual position of wanting them to be beefed up. Some people I knew were happy to do this for me. Maybe they got a kickback from the taxman. They didn't say. The upshot was that I was accepted as a member of the union.

I was never a joiner so it wasn't something I aspired to. I resolved never to go to the meetings and I held good to that promise. I agreed with Hemingway that writing was best done in the privacy of your room rather than going to meetings about it.

On the evenings I wasn't out I spent a lot of my time watching DVDs of old movies. Keith got me in on them. He dealt with a lady in Maine who sold them to him at a few dollars a go. When she retired I asked her if she'd sell me her collection. She said she would have but she didn't have it anymore. When she was moving to her retirement home the truck carrying her collection skidded on a bad road and they were all destroyed.

There was a man in Canada that I tracked down who collected old movies. I bought a stack of them from him. He described them as 'film noirs.' That was just a fancy way of describing what we called gangster films when I was growing up.

My favourite decade was the forties. I loved black and white films, probably because I hadn't seen that many of them in my childhood. Colour had started to come in around the late fifties. I always thought there was something bland about it. The sixties and seventies were even more bland. I didn't order any films from these decades from my dealer. It was nice to know what went on before you were born. I mainly ordered dramas and whodunits - or 'whodidits' as my Aunt Nellie called them. They didn't have to be masterpieces. It was the atmosphere I was after. Many of them were just chewing gum for the eyes.

They relaxed me at night-time. Maybe it was like my mother reading me a bedtime story as a child. Nothing much changed in any of our lives as we grew up. We just put different names on things. A teacher I worked with told a pupil to stop sucking her thumb one day. Later in the day I saw him smoking a cigarette. 'You're doing the same thing,' I said. 'I'll get you for that,' he said.

I found my concentration drifting at work. When that happened the children copped it. They were still doing their psychology on me, working out how far they could go before I'd snap. Sometimes making me snap became a kind of game to them.

I did my best to teach them but sometimes I felt I was irrelevant in the classroom. What did it matter whether I taught them or someone else did? They'd graduate anyway, or fail to. There were probably only about two or three people in any given class you could mould. The others were going to do what they did regardless of your influence. Maybe it was true what people said – primary teachers were only glorified babysitters.

In the evenings I continued to play bad snooker in the leagues. We travelled all over Dublin for our games. Not all of the venues were salubrious. I played against sharks with mad eyes in grimy pubs and clubs. They knew every trick in the book to bustle you. They'd cough or belch as you were about to take a shot or else they'd start a conversation with one of their friends to put you off.

Sometimes they juggled up the points on the scoreboard. You had to watch them like a hawk. Every ball was blood. Playing the away games was twice as hard as the home ones. They had that extra man in the crowd to gee them on. They'd call you out on a push shot or a false foul. They might give in eventually but they'd usually win the game. Their tactics always unsettled me. 'I haven't been practising much,' they'd say as they were signing the dockets after the game. Later on you'd hear from one of their friends that they'd just installed a table in their house, that they had to be scraped off it every night.

Many of them were drinkers. I drank a lot on those nights too. With a pint in your hand you felt you could do the impossible. Just like big drinkers think they're good drivers, they also think they're great snooker players – until they miss a sitter (or hit a bollard.)

The worse I played, the more I believed in myself. Some nights I felt I couldn't miss if I tried. I was God. Once in a blue moon I even won a match.

The drink steadied me. It made me brave. I wasn't walking a greased tightrope with it. It fired me up with a crazy kind of enthusiasm, blotting out all the mistakes of the past.

I was the only one on the team with a car. I ferried everyone to the away venues. Some of them joked that it was the only reason I was kept on. It was like the situation in Delta-K. You got a place on the team not because you were good but because you turned up or because you brought people places.

We propped up the end of the table every season. One year we won but I wasn't playing. I had the flu. Maybe that's why we won. I got a Subs trophy as a consolation prize. It has a statue of a snooker player on it. I still have it. When people admire it I don't go into the details of how I got it. I don't tell them I was lying in bed sick when we won. I had to face the fact that I was more use to the team as a patient than as a player. The greatest favour I ever did them was not turning up.

One of the whizzkids took my place. He didn't look like he was long out of the cradle but he gobbled up everyone he came up against. At that age nobody knows what fear is. They haven't experienced defeat so they laugh at the threat of it. Their bravado makes their opponents nervous, which doubles their advantage.

The trophy meant more to me than to the people who actually played to win it. They were good at the game so they took success for granted. I never won anything before so it became that much more precious to me. I gave it pride of place in the attic. Up there nobody but me could see it. I had at least that much integrity. I loved looking at the gilt figure bent over the table, his frame like the frame of a cue itself. It probably should have been a statue of a car instead of a snooker player. That was my main contribution to the team that year – my wheels.

I kept playing even though I wasn't getting any better. It was the same as I'd been with the guitar years ago. I reached a certain standard with that too and couldn't get beyond it. I gave up the guitar but I refused to give up snooker. I played more and more in the hope that one day I'd start to improve. Even after I lost my place on the team I kept playing. I became a sub. If one of the other players couldn't play a match for some reason I filled in. If you didn't field a full team the other club got a walkover. We didn't want that. There was always the chance I might hit a purple patch, or draw someone of even more limited ability than myself.

I offered my services for a charity match one year. It was for the Rape Crisis Centre. The more balls you potted the more money you raised for it. My match took place on the night before I was due to go to Wales on my summer holidays. I was getting the ferry from Rosslare to Fishguard the next morning so I had to play through the night.

I hated early sailings but in those days I was getting free trips from the ferry company so I had to take what I was given. I used to write puffs for them in a magazine I was working for at the time. You got a courtesy trip if you said they were the greatest company in the world. That was easy enough to do.

My match started at 9 p.m. and went on until 4 in the morning. I didn't pot many balls. My mind wasn't on the games. It was on the trip down to Rosslare that I had to make in a few hours. I always hated going anywhere in the dark. After the match finished I went home and had a cold shower. I drove like the clappers to Wexford. My eyes were falling out of my head. I'd have fallen asleep at the wheel if I didn't leave the windows of the car open. Thankfully there was a wind blowing.

The ferry was getting ready to take off when I reached Rosslare. For a few minutes I thought they weren't going to let me on. As soon as I got onto it I plonked myself over a sofa. I went into one of the deepest sleeps I ever had in my life. I was in the land of nod all the way across the Irish Sea. I woke up around noon and felt weird. I kept thinking of all my missed blacks rather than the poor rape victims. I doubted they made much out of me that night. Maybe ten minutes of counselling on a helpline.

When I got back to the school in the autumn my mind was a million miles away. The children became more demanding as my life drifted away from them. They began to drain me, taking away the reason I went into teaching in the first place. Were they at fault or was I? I didn't know. Maybe I was just getting older.

Teaching was the only job I knew that got harder as it went on. The children's energy level stayed the same but mine dropped. I felt like Glenn Ford in *The Blackboard* Jungle.

My classes were always noisy. Now they became noisier than ever. I stopped being able to deal with it. Sometimes I found myself roaring at the kinds to tone it down. When I did that it only made things worse. If you roar at a child there's a chance he'll roar back. There's a bigger chance he'll lose respect for you because he'll know you're losing control. The manuals said to love the badness out of children. I agreed. It was a noble aspiration. Sadly, I couldn't always achieve it.

Children were seen and not heard when I was a child. If I said I was bored in Ballina I was given a football and told to go out to the back garden or the field up the road. The children of the 1980s were different. When they were bored they acted up. I was expected to 'cure' this by becoming a performing seal. In the child-centred curriculum the children were the lords of the ring, the centre of gravity. The teachers were like their servants.

I started to sleep badly. When I did that, the next day at work was always bad. In the old days teachers could probably have put children doing reading or something basic like that. Modern children were more demanding. They pushed me to my limits.

I kept myself going with black coffees, pinching myself to stay awake till the bell went for the end of the day. Then I'd come home and fall into bed. That night I'd probably be awake for most of the night again because my body clock was disrupted. And so the cycle continued. It was like a nurse coming off night duty to the day shifts. I felt I was in a twilight zone.

I started to come down with bugs. I was up and down to the doctor for tablets every other week to try and get rid of them. I knew my resistance was low. He said it wasn't my immune system that was the problem, it was my stress level. He told me I was in the wrong job, that I was burning myself out.

'You're a perfectionist,' he said.

I thought he was giving me a compliment but he didn't mean it that way. He saw I had elements of OCD, of compulsive behaviour.

'The world isn't perfect,' he said, 'If you think you can make it like that you'll go loopy.'

I dosed myself with every kind of medication going but none of them had any effect. My immune system was so low I was resisting them. Meanwhile at school the kids pounced on any weakness they saw in me. It was like I was on trial every day. There was nowhere to hide in the human zoo they called a classroom.

They were like predators. It was usually the ones you did most for that attacked you when you were down. The ones who didn't need too much education didn't seem to notice.

Something else was bothering me as well. I found myself getting hot flushes when I wore any clothes that were tight to my skin. There were certain fabrics I seemed to have developed an allergy to. I stopped being able to wear shirts that were made of cotton. Silk ones were bearable because they were cold to the touch but they cost a fortune.

I asked Ruth if she could send me some American ones. I felt they'd be light enough considering the climate over there. She said she would but they got lost in the post.

I started looking for them in charity shops. Once in a blue moon I found one. Even then I had to keep them open at the neck. I was never able to close the top button of a shirt. If I did I felt I'd choke. If I had to wear one at a function I'd leave that button open. Keith said to me once, 'Are you trying to look like Frank Sinatra?'

Alex Higgins was a bit like me. He was the only snooker player who was allowed play the game without a bow tie. He got a letter from his doctor to say it irritated his throat. I'd have been looking for a similar letter in the unlikely event that I ever reached Higgins' level of snooker. Actually I never really believed he had that irritation. I thought he pulled the tie off as part of the drama he liked carrying around with him.

The heat of my body always seemed to be centred on my Adam's apple. The only way around the problem in the long term was to stop wearing shirts altogether. I put a jumper over my vest and left it at that. I also had problems with jumpers. I couldn't

112

wear round-necked ones. They had to be V-necked to keep the wool away from my neck.

Was this all part of my stress too? Was the job to blame? I didn't know. My mind was out to lunch a lot of the time. I stopped caring how the pupils performed. It was as if I was giving my classes to myself. I felt like a ham actor rehearsing lines nobody would ever hear. I was an unnecessary person in the room. When I gave orders they seemed to be coming from someone else, from a part of my psyche that I wasn't even acquainted with anymore. If I told them to keep off the grass or to learn off an irregular verb I wasn't thinking about these things. I was thinking of how many more days of torture I'd have to put in until the holidays arrived.

The last straw came the day the prefab went up in flames. I felt it was deliberate. I was refereeing a game of football when I saw the smoke. I rushed back but it was too late. It went up like a tinderbox. One of my pupils admitted he was at fault. He said he'd flicked a match into a cupboard without realising it was lit.

He wasn't someone I'd had a problem with, or at least a problem I knew about. He was one of the people who came to the Phoenix Park to cheer me on when I ran the marathon. Had I been too hard on him as a teacher? If I had, this was his revenge.

As I watched the flames rise into the sky I felt somebody up there was trying to tell me something. He was trying to tell me I should never have become a teacher.

Fires in schools happened in New York. They happened in London. Maybe they even happened in Dublin, at least in the inner city. They didn't happen in cosy little villages in the countryside

'Look on the bright side,' the principal said, 'You'll probably have a nice holiday for yourself now.'

113

Eleven

Stories about priests and Christian Brothers abusing young boys in their care started to appear in the newspapers as we got into the new decade. In 1992 the Eamon Casey story broke. He'd fathered a child by an American woman but didn't want anything to do with it. The nation was shocked, not only by the sexual element but also by the fact that he'd misappropriated diocesan funds to pay for the upkeep of the child.

At least the sex was consensual, and with an adult. A few years later we heard about the shocking abuses committed by Brendan Smyth on children.

They seemed to open a floodgate of revelations as the millennium ground to a close. It was as if someone opened a cupboard and everything tumbled out. Why hadn't people spoken up before? Were they afraid? Had they repressed it? I would have known all about that. I'd done the same with Creeper.

The relating of the abuses became like a tsunami once that first silence was broken. There was even an abuser in Ballina. It was our music teacher in Primary School. I hadn't known he was that way inclined when he taught me. I was one of the lucky ones.

I saw programmes on television about traumatised children. Some of them took their own lives in adulthood. Others pursued litigation. They were dragged through the courts in drawn-out cases where lawyers used every trick in the book to get their clients off.

Many priests were moved to other parishes when their abuse was uncovered. Some of them were shipped overseas to continue it. It wasn't only in Ireland the abuses took place. There were equally shocking stories in America, Australia, anywhere you looked. A vast catalogue of Irish names seemed to crop up no matter what the country was.

Attendances at Mass trailed off. Some people went so far as to renounce their Catholicism. Others didn't bother. Many people lost their faith. Was this a reaction to the scandals? I couldn't understand that side of it. They were blaming God for the bad priests. It reminded me of the Beckett line from *Malone Dies*, 'The bastard! He doesn't exist!'

Not all of the children were victims of the clergy. A large number of the lay population were abusers as well. Many of the children had been abused in their homes by their fathers. These people sought out the counsel of the best lawyers. My father would have turned in his grave reading about the horrors that unfolded. So would my mother. It wasn't even hinted at during their lifetimes.

I wondered what might have happened if Creeper abused me sexually. I'd hardly have told anyone about it if he had. If I did, would they have believed me? One of my brothers had been touched by an old man in a cinema one day. He ran home and told my father. He wanted to have him arrested but my mother was against it. In the end they dealt with the man himself. He got a warning that if it happened again they'd bring him to court.

The incidences of abuse were staggering in their numbers. They'd taken place everywhere – in homes, in schools, in the corridors of power. More often than not the abusers had someone protecting them. That's why they went undetected so long.

It wasn't enough for one person to blow a whistle. He wouldn't be listened to. Sometimes you were better to say nothing. If you spoke up you were 'that person.' People labelled you with it. What good was their sympathy? Now you'd have another scar to add to the abuse one – the fact that everyone in the country knew about you.

I was comfortable with my silence. If I kept quiet long enough, I told myself, the memory of anything I suffered might go away in time.

The fact that I wasn't over Creeper was made blindingly clear to me one night when I was in a bar with one of the other teachers I worked with. We were discussing a case that had been in the paper about a priest that abused a child. He'd been abusing him for years before it came to light. The teacher said to me, 'If it was my child, I'd have killed the bastard.' Without thinking I said, 'There are worse things than sexual abuse. There are even worse things than violence.'

He looked at me as if he couldn't believe what he was hearing. He said, 'What's that supposed to mean?' My face went red. I didn't want to say anything to him about my past. If I did I knew he'd never stop pestering me about it. Before long it would have been all over the school. 'I don't know what I meant,' I said, 'You're right. These people need to be put away. If it was my child I'd probably kill the person who did it as well.'

Drink made me think about him more. It brought up things about him that I thought I'd forgotten – his smile, the way he stood over me, the steely look that came into his eyes as he reached for his stick. Most people had heard stories of abuse victims who took to drink. Some of them even became abusers themselves. Would the day ever come when I'd start hitting my pupils to get something out of myself? I dreaded the thought.

I was forty when I walked out the door of the school for the last time in 1993. It was a good age to begin Part Two of my life – at least if I didn't drink too much. Teaching carried the temptation of the pub from 2.30 onwards. Being a writer meant you could start much sooner. At breakfast, for instance.

One of my colleagues rang Mary without telling me. 'Does Aubrey know what he's doing?' he said to her. It was thoughtful of him to do that but the question wasn't relevant. When you were in the wrong job you had to get out whether you knew what you were doing or not. If I didn't I felt I'd end up in the funny farm.

The *Evening Press* closed down the following year. It was a big blow for me. I was now trapped as a union member, paying a sub every month with nothing to show for it. The NUJ didn't get you work. It just took your money. I didn't see the point of being in it but I'd had such a job getting in I was slow to leave it. If I did and another job came along I might find it hard to be re-accepted. Someone told me they were coming down hard on freelancers even if you only did the odd nixer. They could cut off your blood supply.

Two other things happened that year that had enormous repercussions on the world. The first was Liz Hurley wearing her safety pin dress to the premiere of *Four Weddings and a Funeral.* It caused all sorts of questions to be asked throughout the world. How long was it going to take her to get into it? What if she stabbed herself? More importantly, how long would it take Hugh Grant to get it off? We knew how passionate he was from his adventures with Divine Brown on Sunset Boulevard.

The second event that made the year reverberate was the trial of O.J. Simpson. I watched it non-stop. I even moved the television into another room for it. It became known as The O.J. Room.

I became consumed with the idea that he had to be found guilty. My mind couldn't comprehend the fact that he wouldn't. When the acquittal verdict was announced I couldn't take it in. It didn't make sense to me. It was only later I came to accept the fact that guilty black people had the right to be found innocent just as guilty white ones had been for so many decades. It was poetic justice – revenge for Rodney King. And all the other Rodney Kings.

After it was over I couldn't stop thinking about it. I wrote a letter to Marcia Clark, Simpson's prosecutor, to tell her how devastated I felt for her. I also wrote to Christopher Darden, her fellow prosecutor, to tell him he was wrong to ask O.J. to put on the glove that was discovered at Simpson's Brentwood home in the aftermath of the murders. With his blood on it. It shrunk over time, leading to Johnny Cochrane's famous mantra, 'The glove don't fit, you must acquit.'

I also wrote letters to Robert Shapiro, Mark Fuhrman and Barry Scheck. I even thought of sending one to Kato Kaelin, the guy who lived with Simpson at the time of the murders. And to Dennis Fung for mucking up the DNA evidence.

Twelve

I wrote a biography of Elvis Presley in 1997. I'd read dozens of books on him and planned to make my one different. It was meant to be a fan book too but I didn't want to sanitise him.

Because it was the twentieth anniversary of his death it had some 'topspin.' John Kavanagh, a friend of mine from the Elvis Social Club, helped me with it. He was an Elvis impersonator as well as a DJ. His speciality was the song 'The Wonder of You.' He liked messing with the words. 'When no one else can understand me,' he sang, 'When everything I do is wrong/You give me hope and constipation.'

Every week or so we went down to Bachelor's walk and made fools of ourselves pretending to be trains (for 'Mystery Train') or throwing scarves into non-existent audiences *a la* Elvis or saying 'uh-huh' out of the side of our mouths. most of the people knew the names of almost every song he'd recorded and almost every line of dialogue he'd ever spoken in his films. They'd have been much better candidates to write a book on him if they were bothered to but they weren't.

We launched it in a pub in Frances Street. Most of the people from the Social Club were there. John talked about it from the stage but nobody listened to him. There was a problem with the sound system. Then he introduced me. I talked about it but nobody listened to me either. I was glad about that.

People proceeded to get drunk. I sat at a table with a pile of my books. Every so often someone would come up and take one. They stuffed money down my jumper. When I stood up it fell to the ground. A girl with Down's Syndrome kept picking it up for me.

I didn't sign any copies. People asked me to but I hated doing it. I felt it was show-offy. If I was a carpenter and I made a table I wouldn't have put my name on it. What made a book any different? A girl who'd broken her arm asked me to sign the cast. That was all right. It was different. I had a photo of Elvis signing an autograph for a child by putting her notebook on her head. I'm sure he would have approved.

I didn't like dedications on books either. I felt they alienated readers. If I saw something like 'To Richard with love' on the first page of a book I lost interest in it. Why was Richard getting the love and not me? I found myself becoming jealous of him. When Elvis sang, people said, he made you feel like he was singing to you and you alone. A writer should try to have the same relationship with his readers.

At the end of the night I sang a song from the stage. I use the word 'sang' advisedly. I didn't know how bad I was until a few nights later. Someone from the group recorded it and made a tape. He gave it to me as a gift. Gift? With friends like that who needs enemies. It also had footage of me dancing around the bar on Bachelor's Walk pretending to be the train. After watching it I burned it. If there are any more copies of this video on eBay I'd pay good money to have them destroyed. .

Most of the people in the group liked my book but there were some exceptions. One night I was donating some copies of it to a benefit for the disease Friedrich Ataxia. A woman came up to me. She told me she'd burned her one.

'Why?' I asked her.

'I can't forgive you for saying Elvis was a drug abuser,' she said, 'and that he made bad films.'

'Are you for real?' I said, causing her to storm off. What price loyalty? Some people wanted to preserve him as a deity. I didn't think he would have wanted that. 'Cut me and I bleed,' he said, 'I put my legs into my trousers one at a time.'

I found it hard to sleep that night. Everyone knows that if you write a book and 99 people out of 100 praise you for it, the only one you remember is the person who didn't. Anytime I wrote something I thought the world was going to stop when it was published. Maybe all writers are like that. We have God complexes. It tortures us when someone says we're anything less than perfect.

A few nights later I saw that an Elvis impersonator (not John Kavanagh) was about to do a show in a pub in Camden Street. I rang the manager and asked him if he'd allow me to display my book in the pub. He said that would be fine. He set up a table outside the room the show was going to be in. I only had to pay him a small fee.

I expected huge sales but they didn't materialise. I should have remembered what happened in the pub in Frances Street. I can't remember anyone even looking at it that night. They all made straight for the counter. The experience taught me a lesson. It made about as much sense trying to sell a book in a pub as it would have done trying to sell beer in a library.

When I thought about it I came to the conclusion that my book didn't have anything new to say about Elvis. I made a few points about the Irish connection to him but by and large it was a by-numbers confection. Could I do anything about that? I put my thinking cap on.

After a few months I set about writing another book on him, this time from the inside. I knew he'd always wanted to write his autobiography. He was going to call it *Through My Eyes*. He hadn't got around to it but maybe I could. I got the idea of pretending I broke into Graceland one night and found his diaries. What if I became their custodian?

I wrote *The Elvis Diaries* as a day-to-day set of entries. I intended to write some of the pages in his handwriting. I knew how to imitate it.

Would that cause copyright problems? I asked a solicitor I knew for advice. He told me it would. He even suggested I might be sued by Elvis Presley Enterprises, the people who looked after his franchises.

I told him that was ridiculous, that my book was a mockumentary. 'Don't find out the hard way,' he said, 'These people are very protective of their franchises.'

Around this time a man called Sid Shaw who ran a shop in Manchester won a case allowing him to use Elvis' image on memorabilia he was selling. I remembered a similar brouhaha breaking out around O.J. Simpson during his trial some years before. People were flogging fridge magnets and keyrings with his image on them. Had they the right to do that? Had I the right to use Elvis' image? It was a legal minefield. I didn't mind Elvis Enterprises owning his properties but I didn't think they had the right to own the man himself.

There was no point thinking about it too much. It got in the way of the writing. I put my head down and finished doing the book.

I documented Elvis' problems with his manager and his bodyguards. I also wrote about his oedipal relationship with his mother and his addiction to food and prescription pills. I incorporated real events into the fictional parts.

I got a contract for it from a publisher in London. He told me he had an agent who was interested in it. He said he wanted to fly over to Ireland to talk about it.

I met the two of them in a hotel in Sutton. The agent seemed to be a real Elvis fan. He had rare photographs of him and also a lot of memorabilia, including a letter Elvis wrote the day he died. I told him I'd be happy for him to represent me with the book.

He took out a piece of paper and asked me to sign it. He said it was a contract. I signed it without reading it. I was too engrossed in his memorabilia to bother.

It turned out I'd signed away the rights of it to him. He had me over a barrel with it for the next few years. I tried to get them back off him but I was blocked legally.

He took the book to America and showed it to Joe Esposito, Elvis' right hand man. Esposito then showed it to Priscilla Presley, Elvis' widow. Apparently she didn't like it any more than the woman at the Friedrich Ataxia gig liked my original biography. I was informed that if it was published she was going to sue. She hadn't liked what I wrote about the pill-popping or some sexual things. I tried to explain to the agent that this material was in the public domain and indeed included in Priscilla's own autobiography. All I'd done was put it into Elvis' voice.

'I know it sounds crazy,' he said, 'but it has to be done.'

After I did it he said, 'Oh, I forgot to mention. You'll have to do a chapter about the day Elvis killed that guy.'

You could have knocked me over with a feather.

'What are you talking about?' I said.

'You mean you didn't know? He ran him down one day in his car and then left the scene. Parker knew about it. That's why he had such power over him.' I was amazed that he found my writing about the pill-popping inflammatory and yet here he was talking casually about a death.

I adapted the manuscript a third time and the agent went off with it. He told me he'd do everything it took to sell it.

Eventually he did just that, along with some other musical properties he had. He got £100,000 for them.

I didn't see a penny of it and neither did he tell me about it. I discovered it by accident one night when I was surfing the net.

I rang him a few days afterwards to congratulate him on his windfall.

'Thanks,' he said, either not recognizing my sarcasm or not pretending to, 'I spent a lot of it on expenses trying to get your book up and running around the world.'

Sure thing. And Elvis is still alive and well and stacking shelves in a delicatessen somewhere in Winnipeg.

Thirteen

In 1998 I decided to write a biography of Ernest Hemingway. The hundredth anniversary of his birth was coming up the following year. I thought it would be a nice tie-in. The fact that I'd done an 18,000 thesis on him for my M.A. was surely going to be a help, I thought. At least if I could find it. It was thirteen years since I'd done it. I wasn't in the habit of keeping things like that longer than thirteen minutes.

I rang UCD to ask them if they had a copy of it.

The person on the end of the phone said, 'Drop in to see us.'

When I got there I was ushered in to a little room by a dapper little man. His expression seemed to say, 'You must be mad.'

Approximately 5000 bound theses sat looking up at me in various stages of disarray.

'Is there no filing system?' I said to him.

'What does it look like?' he said.

I spent an hour digging through various tomes on everyone from Dickens to Anthony Trollope. I didn't find my masterpiece. When I asked the man if he knew of any other copies anywhere he said, 'Manchester, maybe.'

His attitude confirmed a suspicion I always had, i.e. universities didn't care about their students' theses any more than the students did. The revelation came as something of a relief.

My book came out the following year. We missed the centenary by a month. It was my first experience of a publishing cock-up.

One of the themes of the book was, yet again, that of the loser. Most writers, I thought, were losers in life. They performed exorcisms on the page that acted as catharses for them – if they were lucky.

Maybe W.B. Yeats was the classic example of this. If he hadn't been a loser in love, would he have been able to write all those powerful poems about Maud Gonne MacBride? His loss was literature's gain. The lover that gets away spurs the imagination much more than the one people have and hold. The worlds of literature and music would hardly exist without loss. Can you think of a love song that ends happily? Off the top of my head I can't, at least one with a story in it.

The love stories both in Hemingway's life and in his books generally ended sadly. He left his first two wives. His third one left him. He wasn't happy with his fourth.

'In the childhood of Judas,' Graham Greene said once, 'Jesus was betrayed.' I spent much of my time writing about his early years in the book. Some of his neuroses began there. His mother dressed him as a girl for the first two years of his life. She'd wanted a daughter. Was he traumatised by that? Did it cause him to over-develop his macho side as a reaction? It was an interesting theory. Gertrude Stein once accused him of wearing false hairs on his chest. Other writers also castigated him for being faux-macho. And a bully.

I wasn't sure where I stood on the debate. I knew his hatred of his mother fed into a lot of his fiction. I thought it gave him, by extension, a hatred of anything associated with domesticity. She was what Aunt Sally was to Huckleberry Finn. *Huckleberry Finn* was one of Hemingway's favourite books.

Maybe he pushed things too far. If you denied the feminine side of your nature it could come back to haunt you. That happened to him in his last years when he turned into a neurotic. He became terrified the FBI were out to get him. He'd buried a part of himself for most of his life and now it was taking him over. It was like the 'Mother' side of Norman Bates in

Psycho. That might sound like an exaggeration but anyone who read about Hemingway's last years knew how far off the edge he went.

I'd taken on the project expecting it to be just another book. The deeper I got into it the more I realised I knew practically nothing about the man when I'd been doing my thesis on him in UCD. I hadn't even know he'd written a novel in the forties based on the theme of cross-dressing. It was called *The Garden of Eden* and was unpublished at the time of his death. Some readers of his books saw evidence of androgyny in all of them, including *For Whom the Bell Tolls*.

Maybe the most amazing thing I learned on this score wasn't about Hemingway at all but rather about his son Gregory. At his father's funeral Gregory met a woman called Valerie Danby-Smith, an *Irish Times* journalist who'd become his secretary for the last two years of his life. At this point Gregory was a doctor. He married Valerie and she had four children by him. Then he started to cross-dress. One night he was arrested for vagrancy when police saw him wandering down a Florida street in a confused state. He was in a woman's dress at the time. He died later that night in the woman's section of a jail.

I wanted to pursue this theme in more detail in my book. I discovered Valerie was still alive. I managed to get her phone number from a Hemingway scholar so I rang her.

She seemed curious when she picked up the phone. I told her I was writing a book on Hemingway and would appreciate it if she helped me with it.

She went quiet for a few moments. Then she said, 'How did you get this number?' I told her. 'What's your name?' she asked me. As I said it I could hear her writing it down. Then she hung up.

I learned later that as well as having four children by Gregory, Valerie also had one by Brendan Behan.

I almost jumped out of my chair when I read that. So Hemingway and Behan were related through marriage. It beggared belief.

Valerie, who was now going by the name Valerie Hemingway, went on to write a book that contained all this information, *Running with the Bulls*. It was fascinating. I wish it was published earlier. I could have used it for my research. It would have given a whole different complexion to my book.

The other thing that shocked me in my research was how much suicide there was in Hemingway's life. Apart from his father killing himself, so did his brother Leicester, his sister Ursula and possibly his other sister Marcelline. His father-in-law (Hadley Richardson's father) had also killed himself, and his grand-daughter Margaux. His son Jack once said, 'I want to die naturally. I want to see how long a Hemingway can live by natural means.'

When the new millennium came in I told myself I was going to create a new me. That meant ridding myself of all my demons, including my clerical ones. I felt that would be easier now that we were living in a more enlightened country. Modern Ireland, we were told by the chattering classes of Dublin 4, had all the answers. It had shackled off the coils of Mother Church.

Life was definitely more secularised. Pundits on television programmes said trendy things like 'We're living in a post-Catholic society.' The priests who once owned us, who terrorised us, became negligible figures. Some of them got married. Many were laicised. Some were spat at on the street.

I felt nostalgic for the past, fearful for the future. I found myself becoming alienated from holier-than-thou people but even moreso from those who said things like, 'I don't believe in a God with a white beard but I think there's something out there.' It was like, 'Beam me up, Scottie.' Such people started to immerse themselves in things like Rastafarianism, Kabbalah, Tarot cards. I was reminded of G.K. Chesterton's statement, 'When people stop believing in God they don't replace him with nothing. They replace him with anything.'

Was this free-thinking or just another form of sheepishness? In the fifties we all followed the establishment. In the nineties we junked it. We were still joining the pack. 'Our churches are being turned into shopping centres,' someone said, 'In the next generation maybe our shopping centres will be turned back into churches.'

Everyone gets their day in the sun. As someone who wanted to blow the works on the church's dominance in my twenties, I was now having mine. The irony was that I didn't want to now. Like Creeper I'd mellowed. I wasn't someone who chewed the altar rails but I was more accepting of everyone's right to have their views as long as I was allowed to have mine.

Did I make too much of the problems of my adolescence? Probably. In 1965 I went into the eye of the storm. In 1969 I came out of it. So what? Nobody died. A man hit me a few punches. Did that justify thirty years of obsessing about him and the culture he represented? I put some of my obsessions into my writing. Maybe I needed them for that reason.

My Prion editor Andrew Goodfellow came to Ireland to attend the wedding of the writer Joe O'Connor. He was Sinead's brother. I'd met him briefly in the BBC studio in London when I was promoting *Hollyweird*. We were both waiting to be interviewed and fell into conversation. Not really thinking about what I was saying, I asked him how he felt about nepotism. I don't think he was too impressed.

I met Andrew in O'Dwyers, the famous Joyce pub. We discussed the prospect of me doing a biography of

Jimmy White. We'd talked a lot about him over the years. He felt there was a book there. Jimmy had already done his autobiography some years before. It was called *Behind the Eight Ball,* a pun on the American expression 'behind the white ball.' He'd done it with a co-writer. I'd applied for the job but it was given to a lady called Rosemary Kingsland instead.

I didn't think she did a very good job. The first thing you have to get right in a co-writing job is the voice of your subject. This Kingsland manifestly failed to do. Her style was so ornate, at one point I expected her to say something like 'I espied an individual in a game-playing auditorium.' I felt I was reading a book by Auberon Waugh when it should have sounded more like Damon Runyon.

Andrew had his girlfriend with him. She listened avidly to our conversation, occasionally chipping in suggestions. One of them was that the book should be called *Modesty Baize.* This was another pun – on the Dirk Bogarde film *Modesty Blaise.* I thought it was a great idea. Jimmy was nothing if not modest.

I made many efforts to get going on the book in the next few months, dredging up every experience I could think of to make it work. The idea was that it would be a book that was as much about me as Jimmy. Andrew was in favour of that. To help it along he sent me a few books in the post. One of them was *A Fan's Notes* by Frederick Exley. It was about Exley's obsession with the New York Giants. Another was Davis Miller's *The Tao of Muhammad Ali.* This was like a new genre. It sounded interesting but I wasn't able to master it. No matter how hard I tried I couldn't muster up enough material to make the idea work. We decided to park it for a few years until I felt ready to do it justice.

Afterwards I got the idea of doing a book on Charles Bukowski, one of the world's most famous alcoholics. I didn't know much about him at the time. His books weren't prescribed on any of my UCD courses. Universities didn't like him despite the fact that he often read his work in them. Or maybe because of that. He usually disgraced himself at the readings.

He was too straightforward for anyone to do a thesis on him. He reminded me of Oscar Wilde's dictum, 'I live in terror of being understood.' I saw the parallels to Hemingway right off but he had something Hemingway didn't have – humour.

I wrote to John Martin, his publisher at Black Sparrow Press in Santa Rosa. Martin had discovered him, paying him a monthly fee to write so he could leave his job in the post office. I asked him if he'd be interested in me doing a collection of Bukowski's sayings. He thought this was a trivial idea so he knocked it on the head. He was probably right but I felt the world could have done with hearing some of his more quotable quotes, like, 'Some people never go crazy. What truly horrible lives they must lead.'

I hadn't thought of doing a biography of him at that stage. Howard Sounes had done what was seen as the definitive one. What could I add to it? There were a few short memoirs out there as well but they didn't seem to have anything Sounes didn't.

The more I read of his work the more I liked it. I'd never seen anything this corrosive in my life. Leonard Cohen said, 'He pulled everything down, even the angels.' He changed my attitude not only to literature but to life. After reading him I knew I'd never be beholden to anyone again. I'd never be intimidated by anyone. I'd never be talked down to by anyone. Maybe I'd never even trust anyone.

He turned everything I knew about life on its head. I'd never heard of anyone who lived like him. It was a miracle he'd survived what he put his body through. A lot of writers talked tough but he was the real deal.

I liked the fact that the Beats didn't embrace him into their fold. After reading Bukowski, even Kerouac started to look like a softie.

Being the youngest of an old-fashioned family from a small town in a conservative country, most of my influences up to now were middle of the road. They were mainstream movies and Rogers & Hammerstein songs. Punk rock passed me by. Grunge passed me by. So did heavy metal and left wing politics.

The fact that my father had affiliations to the British Empire meant I grew up in a political vacuum. He was said to have had a gun pulled on him in a pub one night when he sang 'God Save the Queen.' I grew up believing that the 1916 uprising was just a few stray bullets fired by malcontents on an Easter Monday and then promptly forgotten about.

My rebels were predictable ones like Dylan and Brando and James Dean. Bukowski was in a different league. He'd have eaten these people without salt. The idea of me doing a book on a degenerate barfly whose main female company was alcoholic hookers would probably have had me run out of Ballina.

The fact that I discovered him myself was important to me. Hugo had introduced me to Hemingway. He gave me a copy of *For Whom the Bell Tolls* in the early seventies. That was the book that lit the fuse for me.

Hugo was ahead of a lot of people in Ballina in his tastes. He talked about people like Ingmar Bergman and Fellini. He told us about brilliant films like *Persona* and *Juliet of the Spirits*.

He also introduced me to Albert Camus' *The Outsider*, the most mind-blowing book I ever read. And he introduced me to Norman Mailer. He had a copy of *Advertisements for Myself* in Norfolk. There weren't too many people reading Mailer in Ballina in those days. Maybe there still aren't. He introduced me to Bob Dylan as well. One day in Ballina he came back from Byron's record shop with a copy of *John Wesley Harding* under his arm. It was one of the lesser known Dylan albums.

Basil was another influence on me. He'd gotten me in on James Joyce. I remember him going down to Keohane's bookshop one day and buying *Portrait of the Artist as a Young Man*. *Ulysses* became an obsession with him in later years. He went on to become chairman of the James Joyce Society in New York.

The thing about Bukowski was that he was my discovery. I'd never heard his name mentioned by anyone growing up. Once I started reading him I couldn't stop. My first exposure to him was in the basement of Eason's. It was on a shelf where books that didn't fit into any category were kept. I always liked those kinds of shelves best. It was one of his poetry collections. I can't remember which one. It didn't read like poetry. It was like prose in poetic form. The first poem I read must have gone on for six or seven pages. I was hooked.

I went in search of other books by him. They were hard to come by in those days. Apart from the one I'd just read, Eason's didn't stock them. They didn't even have a way of ordering them from Black Sparrow. After a while I found a shop on the quays called The Forbidden Planet. It sold graphic novels. They said they'd order them for me and they did.

For the next few months I walked down to The Forbidden Planet with a great sense of expectation when they phoned to say they had a new title in. They weren't cheap. Some of them cost over £40 but I'd have paid ten times that amount for them. After I'd got through as many poetry books as I could find I went in search of the novels. They were equally gripping. Then I got the letters and the articles. Did he ever stop writing? How did he do it with all that drink in him?

If his poems blew me away, reading about his life did it on the double. The nightmare upbringing, the *acne vulgaris*, the ten year drunk, nearly dying of a bleeding ulcer in the charity ward of a hospital in 1955, the miraculous comeback – you couldn't make it up.

I found a lot to identify with in my own life. I hated the politics around writing like he did and we both liked the rat-tat-tat of the typewriter. He called it his machine gun. Both of us had also been influenced by Hemingway.

We had something else in common too. We both left jobs that were killing us to become writers. He gave his one up in 1969, the year I left Ballina.

I felt I had to do a book on him. Did I have anything to say that hadn't been said already? Maybe Sounes left some gaps that I could fill in. I wrote in the same frantic way Bukowski did. At one stage I formed the idea that I'd do the whole book in lower case letters. Bukowski often wrote that way, being too lazy (or drunk) to press the Caps key. That proved impractical though. I went for the more conventional option in the end.

After a few months I felt what I'd written would qualify as a sidebar to Sounes' book. It was never meant to be anything else. After finding a publisher for it (an offbeat company in Manchester) I wrote to John Martin again. I asked him if he'd give me permission to quote from Bukowski's works.

He said no. Maybe he remembered me from the 'Sayings' idea. I was surprised even if he did. Was he not interested in the publicity my book would generate for his author? Some publishers might have been but he wasn't. I suppose he didn't need me. Anything Bukowski wrote had gone viral by now.

Martin had got rich on him. Any writings by people like me weren't going to buffet that by much.

I wasn't used to being blocked like that. I didn't have such problems with my Hemingway book. When I rang the Library of Congress they provided me with all the visual material on Hemingway that I wanted. They also said I could use it without attribution or cost. I didn't expect Martin to accord me such largesse when it came to the thorny subject of illustrations.

A man in Newcastle offered me the right to quote from an anthology of Bukowski's work that he'd edited. That was good news but my publisher wanted to bring the book out in a joint UK/US edition and the man from Newcastle only had permission for the quotations in the British Isles. I ended up not being able to use them. The book suffered as a result of that as I'd already inserted the quotes into my text. Now I had to take them all out again. It meant many paragraphs lost their 'meat.'

The book only sold modestly. Bukowski audiences are a tough crowd. They don't take kindly to people like me jumping on his bandwagon. A lot of them thought I did it for the money. Some reviewers on Amazon took it apart. I was accused of being a grave-digger, an exploiter of his memory.

Seeing words like 'necrophiliac' applied to me cured me of reading reviews of my books on Amazon. People who don't know anything about authors character assassinate them on book sites like this. Some writers are driven to suicide by the negative publicity they get on these platforms. They're filled with the demented mutterings of cynics who get their kicks by pulling people down.

I received the grand sum of £700 for the book. It was a flat fee. There were no royalties. I spent about ten times that amount on my research. So much for being a necrophiliac.

Some of the reviewers pointed out that the production of the book was bad. In that they were right. The font was small. Reading it was like looking through a telescope backwards. Other reviews said my style of writing was over the top. They were right about that too. I was too immersed in the man to see my prose for what it was – purple.

Years later I re-wrote the book. A man in San Francisco published it. I toned down the style and added a lot of new material that I'd learned in the intervening years. It made it more solid. That isn't to say there weren't problems with it. I still couldn't quote from his works and I only had a few photographs of him. They were given to me by one of his publishers, the editor of Sun Dog Press in Michigan.

I contacted Howard Sounes to ask him if I could use some of his ones. He was unhelpful. I thought he'd be different. I liked his style of writing and I also liked the subjects of his books. He'd written other ones on Tiger Woods, Bob Dylan and Fred and Rose West. It was the kind of mix I liked. Once again it proved the truth of the old dictum that it's not always a good idea to contact people you admire.

Sounes was versatile. I tried to be too. Most writers I knew had a particular *shtick*. They were poets or novelists. They specialised in biographies or celebrity books, books about sailing or cookery or Polynesian architecture.

I couldn't just do one thing. It would have bored me. If I was an actor I'd have been a character actor rather than a star. If I was a musician I'd have been an eclectic one. The problem with being eclectic is that you didn't build up a fanbase. People never knew what to expect from me, including myself.

I liked a quotation I read from Marlon Brando: 'I become fanatically interested in everything I do for approximately seven seconds.' That was me too.

Fourteen

I went back to Ballina every few years. I used to meet Michael, a friend of mine from across the street. We used to go to The Hibs in the old days. He was running a record shop in King Street now.

He filled me in on all the local news any time I met him. He was two years younger than me. That meant a lot when we were growing up. Now it was negligible.

We talked about the days when we used to play Buddy Holly songs in our front room, when we used to record our voices on my Aunt Mary's tape recorder. It was one of the first ones I ever saw. We were fascinated by its huge spools.

When I moved to Dublin first I lost contact with him. It was interesting to hear him talk about his hippie phase, his trips outside Ireland. After I left the town I had a mental image of everyone I knew being stuck there. It was difficult to envisage them on foreign soil or having the kind of life outside Ballina that I had. That was what memory did to you. It stuck people in the world you inhabited with them when you were in it.

Norfolk was still a community centre. One year when I went in to have a look around I saw a poster saying 'Jerry Cowley – Consultancy Room Upstairs.' Jerry had been in my class in Muredach's. When Butty was asking all of us what we'd do in life one day, Jerry piped up, 'I'm going to be a doctor.' Everyone was surprised as he'd been something of a harem scarem in school. He said he'd never have been able to forgive himself if he saw someone bleeding on the street and wasn't able to help them. Nobody believed him until he went off to UCG to study medicine. That was the university in Galway.

He became involved in politics there. I remember ringing him one day to discover he was in a sit-in protesting against the conditions for the students. Another time, along with a group of like-minded souls, he carried a coffin with 'Democracy' written on it all the way from Galway to Dublin. He practised as a doctor in Mulrany, a village in Mayo, and became highly respected. In fact one year he became Mayoman of the Year.

By now he'd become a politician. He was heavily involved in the Shell to Sea campaign. It opposed the construction of a natural gas pipeline through the parish of Kilcommon in Mayo by Royal Dutch Shell. He'd also started a scheme to help people who'd spent their lives working overseas come home and set up house in Ireland at an affordable rate. It was called Safe Home Ireland.

I knocked on the door of his 'consultancy room.' He was deep in chat with a farmer. I nodded over at him. He recognised me immediately even though we hadn't seen one another in years.

'What are you doing in my parents' bedroom?' I said. He laughed. He'd been in it many times when we were growing up.

We agreed to meet for coffee in the Ridge Pool, a hotel down by the Moy. I told him I'd kept in touch with his career. He didn't know too much about mine. 'I write books for people who move their lips when they read,' I told him, 'I'm not likely to become Mayoman of the Year anytime soon.' He said not to demean myself, that everyone was put on earth for a purpose. Nobody had the right to feel any more important than anyone else.

We talked about the old days, about the times we used to climb in through the barbed wire in the golf links and skelp balls at each other with makeshift clubs. We were basically playing hurley when I thought about it.

'At least you got out of teaching,' he said as we parted.

Maybe I should never have gone into it in the first place. What would have happened if I stayed at Commerce? I'd probably have become an accountant and pursued my hobbies in the evenings. I doubt I'd have stayed at it long. The routine would have killed me.

In the following weeks I started to have a recurring dream about teaching. It was coming close to the end of term and the children were going crazy in the classroom. I was about to have a breakdown but I couldn't think of any other job to go into. Would l I stay or would l I go? The dream always ended before I could make up my mind.

What was behind it? It seemed as if the first half of my life was haunted by Creeper and the second half by Clonsilla. Both dreams involved school. What did that say about me? Was I a case of arrested development? I remembered George Bernard Shaw's definition of a teacher, 'A man among children, a child among men.'

The children of my generation hated school and liked their home life. Today's ones liked school but a lot of them went home to dysfunctional lives. Nobody got it every way. Maybe the next generation would have cross teachers again. They'd probably be people like the pupils I taught, people with little patience for things not going their way. Or people like me for whom the liberal approach to the job didn't work. Then it could flip around again, the generation after that again with kind teachers and casual pupils.

John McGahern said he could never pass a school without feeling a sense of relief. I felt that too. No matter how bored I got after I left, or how frustrated, I knew I'd be worse if I was inside those railings. To that extent I was glad I spent some time inside them.

139

We don't know what happiness is until we experience its opposite. Everything is relative.

I kept writing books. Most of them cost me more money than I got in royalties but that wasn't the problem. I couldn't stop. Jacinta said we never change, we just become more of who we are. That was definitely true for me. I often wondered why she never wrote a book, or any of the other girls in the family. They hadn't gone to college either. Was it sexism on my father's part? They said they didn't want to but that was beside the point. Their generation was conditioned.

All the boys in the family wrote. Clive did a few books on theological themes. Keith was working on one about screenwriters. Hugo wrote plays and songs as well as novels. Basil had many books on the go. I was particularly interested in one he wrote about books nobody reads. I told him it was a great idea. 'Yes,' he said, 'but who'll read it?' I thought of doing one on self-publishing, a subject close to my heart but I had the same problem. Who would publish it?

I never saw Creeper again. I don't know if he's still alive or not. He could be in a nursing home somewhere struggling with his Parkinson's. Or even in his house. Some people go on forever.

His nephew went on to play good football for Mayo but it was never enough for the team to win an All-Ireland. The rivalry with Dublin became fierce. They kept breaking my heart by losing to them. It was like a recap of the situation Muredach's had with Jarlath's, the team we usually lost to when I was there, often due to a lack of self-confidence.

Dublin won many games by the slenderest of margins, often just a point. One time we held a big lead over them only for them to get a draw in the dying minutes. Inevitably they won the replay. Maybe it was true about the curse after all. Or maybe we just weren't good enough. Maybe we didn't have the killer touch. We'd sit back and let them at us. Bernard Brogan would get a goal in injury time just as we were rehearsing our winner's speech.

Mayo's failure to drive home the initiative reminded me of Jimmy White in snooker. He was 14-10 up against Stephen Hendry in the 1994 world final and he still went out into the night a beaten man, losing ten frames on the spin. I cracked my hand off a lampshade in anger that night. There was internal bleeding. I had to go to the hospital to have it attended to. 'How did it happen?' the doctor asked me. I didn't know what to say. 'Just one of those Jimmy White accidents you probably see a lot?'

Was he afraid to win? Maybe. Maybe Mayo were too. Nobody denied the fact that Jimmy had the talent to win a world title or that Mayo shouldn't have won an All-Ireland. What was stopping them? Some kind of mental block? It was the only answer.

Jimmy was elbowed out of the 1994 final by Hendry's coolness. Mayo often trod the same path due to poor judgment. How many times had they lost possession of the ball by being bundled off it by the Dubs? How often had they snatched defeat out of the jaws of victory? Eventually I started betting against them just like I had with Jimmy. The money I got from their defeats acted like a consolation to me.

Hendry dominated the nineties just as Davis had had the eighties. Like most players he was intimidated by Davis at the beginning of his career. When he got over that he started to beat him. He did me a favour by taking Davis out time and again but he was never one of my heroes. I don't know why. It was probably his personality. He didn't have the fragility of Jimmy or Higgins. That was what created the excitement. You never knew what they were about to do. Maybe they didn't either.

Hendry beat Jimmy in four world finals. After he lost the 1994 one he said, 'He's beginning to annoy me.' Me too, Jimmy. He beat him in other rounds at Sheffield over the years but never in a in a final. That was where he had the block.

As Jimmy's form faded, Ronnie O'Sullivan appeared on the scene. He was snooker's especial prodigy, the greatest talent the game ever saw or would ever see. He once made a 147 in less than five minutes. Steve Davis sometimes used to spend that long chalking his cue.

Now I had a new hero to follow. Ronnie won too much for my mad scheme of putting money on the guy I wanted to lose to continue working. I lost all the money I made on Jimmy betting against him. Now and again he went kamikaze and gave me a windfall.

I had an account with Paddy Power that allowed me to stake bets at any hour of the day or night. This was manna from heaven to a nocturnal animal like me. If he was winning 4-0 in a best-of-nine coming up to midnight I could place a bet on the other guy at odds of something like 100/1. That used to settle my nerves in case the worst scenario unfolded. Often it did.

I met Ronnie one day in Tallaght when he was over here on a holiday. He turned out to be a very chilled out guy. He wasn't as intense as Jimmy. When I asked him how he did what he did he just shrugged his shoulders. He seemed almost bored by his gift. Making a good lasagne, he said, was as fulfilling to him as winning a world title. Maybe that's the tragedy of life. None of us get the things we want.

At the end of our meeting he said he needed to get to the airport in a hurry. I was amazed when he asked me to drive him. I'd never had a world champion in the car before. When we were on the way he rang his father. Ronnie Senior had been imprisoned in 1992 for killing Bryan Kray, the brother of the Kray twins, in a Chelsea bar. Ronnie always insisted in was self-defence but he still got a lengthy sentence.

He was the main man behind Ronnie's success, having driven him to all his tournaments as a lad. It affected him deeply to see him going 'inside.' Ronnie would go on to capture the seedy world his father inhabited in a series of novels he wrote. It was also a world he inhabited himself for a time, the world that seemed to cause him problems with alcohol and depression for a time.

I finally wrote my biography of Jimmy in 2009. It was, as Andrew Goodfellow suggested, as much about me as him. That was the idea. The publisher didn't go for Andrew's suggested title of *Modesty Baize*, preferring the more straightforward *Whirlwind* instead.

I started it by saying I was a member of a society called Snooker Players Anonymous. This was like Alcoholics Anonymous except the members were suffering from an addiction to snooker instead of booze. I went on to write about the time I tried to meet Jimmy in Goff's when he was being managed by Gary Miller-Cheevers, nearly getting Hugo and myself killed when I ploughed into a ditch on the way home. Other equally ridiculous events followed, like when I had to go to hospital with my cracked fist after Jimmy missed that crucial black at 17-all in the 1994 world final with Stephen Hendry.

A sizeable portion of the book was about Jimmy's rivalry with Steve Davis. In one chapter I referred to Jimmy as The Adrenophile and Davis as The Somnambulist. I said Jimmy felt about Davis like Macbeth felt about the king in that play. 'And under him my genius is rebuked,' I wrote, 'as 'tis said Marc Antony's was by Caesar.'

I could only imagine what Jimmy would feel like as he read those words – if he ever did. He'd probably have said something like, 'This geezer is mad. He needs to be locked up.' I couldn't imagine him having read much Shakespeare. Barry Hearn once said of him, 'He could work out the odds on a three cross double in ten seconds but he doesn't know the capital of France.'

I read somewhere that his teacher made a deal with him when he was in elementary school that if he agreed to come to school in the morning he'd give him every afternoon off. This was an unbelievable concession by the educational system. It was one I doubted was ever applied to any pupil before or since. I wouldn't have minded offering it to some of the headbangers in my class in Clonsilla. The reason it was suggested was because he played truant so often, the school realised they were going to have to make some compromise if they were to get him in there at all.

I was looking forward to seeing the book on the shelves. The publisher made a lovely job of it with a great cover and a fabulous illustrated section inside. Unfortunately he went bankrupt just before it came out. He sent me some copies of it but I never got any royalties. Neither had I been given an advance. It was like something that might have happened to Jimmy himself growing up in Tooting. His world was inhabited by people living on the edge.

I met him a few years ago when he was doing an exhibition match in my local snooker hall in Harmonstown. I wasn't sure if he remembered me from the interview in Goff's or the one in the Kadeen Hotel. I went up to him after the exhibition and gave him a miniature snooker table as a gift. He didn't say if he'd read my book or not and I didn't ask him. I read somewhere afterwards that he didn't like it. When a girl at an exhibition he was doing asked him to sign it he didn't want to. He told her it was put together from newspaper cuttings. I was disappointed to read that. The real reason he didn't like it, I believe, is because I exposed his demons. That probably hurt him too much.

Sone people told me I should have asked his permission before I wrote it but I've never liked doing that. It causes problems with who you're writing about. They don't want this in and they don't want that in. Unauthorised biographies are more reliable because they give warts and all profiles of their subjects.

He pulled off a few spectacular shots that night. The audience got excited watching him but there wasn't much consistency in his play. I felt his game was close to petering out. I felt sad thinking of him as he used to be, potting them from the lampshades. He said he'd go on playing as long as he could see the table and I believed him. In some ways he looked happier than when he was at his peak. Maybe that's the tragedy of all our lives. We can't appreciate the good times until they're gone.

So he's going to keep playing as long as he can see the table. Great. I hope that applies to Ronnie too.

Hendry is different. He retired when he started to slide down the rankings. It's like the difference between John McEnroe and Bjorn Borg in tennis. Borg retired in 1980 after McEnroe beat him at Wimbledon. He said he didn't want to be Number 2. McEnroe said to him, 'Being number 2 is a lot better than being Number 22.' Borg disagreed.

Federer is more like McEnroe than Borg. He doesn't care what number in the world he is as long as he wins matches. I imagine he won't retire until he's about 78.

Maybe it's all down to how much you love what you do. Playing is an end in itself for Jimmy and McEnroe. I'm a bit like that too. I never got to be Number 1 in the world so I wouldn't know what a slide down the rankings feels like but in my own tinpot way I experienced the devastation of defeat that world champions go through.

I played a game in a seedy dive in Crumlin one night which illustrates that. I was taking a long time over a shot.

My opponent said, 'Get a move on, mate. It's not the world championship.' I said, 'To me it is.'

Mary's mother grew up in Galway. Her father was from Cork. She often said to her that if Galway were winning a match you could never count Cork out but it didn't work the other way round. If Galway were losing they dropped their heads and Cork ran the clock down.

Maybe it was the same with Mayo and Dublin. You could never count Dublin out. Brogan would always nip in to score that goal at the death.

For the next few years I was like flotsam and jetsam, writing any kind of thing at all to keep busy. I wrote a collection of poetry and then a book about spirituality in films. There were also a few quotation anthologies and a book on censorship.

I wrote some books for a Welsh firm called Ylolfa Cyf. I'd been over to Wales so often I felt I should take up citizenship there. I'd been up and down the country so much I knew nearly every crack in the roads. The people were friendly and the scenery was to die for. In many ways it was like Ireland.

Ylolfa was tucked away in a village called Talybont. It looked more like a barn than a publishing house. It was presided over by Lefi Gruffudd. He was the last in a scion of Gruffudds. Lefi always made me feel welcome except on the days after Ireland beat Wales in rugby. He made great tea. You could trot a mouse across it.

I started by doing some humour books for him. Afterwards I graduated to one about Welsh alcoholics. It wasn't too difficult to research that. There were almost as many of them as Irish ones.

When Ray Milland played one in *The Lost Weekend* his friends said, 'Is this your life story?'

The last book I did for Lefi was a biography of Tom Jones. The original idea was that I'd write it just about Tom's sexual exploits. I felt that would have been a bit unfair. Nobody could deny that his bed-hopping was second only to that of Hugh Hefner but the fact was that he had a voice as well as a libido. The finished book took it all in.

I liked going to Wales. It was easy to get there. The ferry was only twenty minutes down the road from where I lived.

By now I'd stopped flying. A vomit bucket to Jersey some years before had cured me of that. It shook so much I felt I was getting electric shocks every five seconds. It was a miracle we touched down in one piece.

I'd flown to America four times in the seventies. On all four flights I was a white knuckler. I always suffered from vertigo. I got it on thick carpets or licking air mail stamps. People said it went back to when we were monkeys, when we were afraid of falling from trees. I don't know about that. I can't remember being a monkey. I can hardly remember what I did yesterday.

Valium didn't help – or whiskey. Anytime the plane rumbled I started thinking of all the films I'd seen as a child where the engine failed. The pilot was usually a rookie. He'd have to be 'talked down' by the ground staff.

Some of us have imaginations and some of us don't. I always thought the worst during a crisis. Bono was on a plane once with Sophia Loren when it was struck by lightning.

'Don't worry,' he said, 'That was just God taking your photograph.'

It was one of the best chat-up lines I ever heard – but of course he wasn't chatting her up. Bono was one of the few happy marriages in the music business. She wouldn't have been interested anyway. She had one of the few happy ones in films.

I wish I could have been as witty as Bono. If I was on a plane that was hit by lightning I'd have jumped out even if I didn't have a parachute.

When 9/11 happened it made things a million times worse. Now I didn't have to just worry about crashing anymore but being hijacked as well. There was also my claustrophobia problem. It was probably associated with the thing I had about clothes being close to my skin.

I hated being confined to a tight space. Planes with outside toilets would have suited me. I refused to go into a lift without a mobile phone. I always felt it would jam on me the day the emergency phone on the wall just happened not to be working.

I got panic attacks on Darts if I was crammed up against people at rush hour. On trains I sat near windows. I liked putting my head out. There were a few times I nearly got decapitated by telegraph poles. Afterwards the authorities stopped letting you do that. They brought in windows that only opened the tiniest bit.

The same thing happened in hotels. You couldn't open them. I asked a hotel manager the reason for this one time. He said, 'Health and safety.' I said, 'What about my mental health?'

I had to be let out of a bus once in the middle of nowhere because the windows wouldn't open. The driver asked me if I was going to get sick. 'Worse,' I told him, as I grabbed my suitcase, 'I'm *not* going to.' It was a relief to get out and smell the grass, to look up at the sky. I must have a bit of Paddy Dillon-Malone's agoraphilia in me.

I told my doctor I got agitated in closed spaces.

'Don't panic,' he said, 'Take a deep breath and count to ten.'

I said, 'What if I'm still agitated when I get to ten?'

He said, 'Then you're entitled to panic.'

Fifteen

As the years went on I devoted myself more and more to writing. It was a solitary life but not a lonely one. Loneliness only afflicted sociable people. I was often asked to do interviews about my books. I tried to get out of as many of these as I could. I knew I was hurting my sales but it was worth it.

I was also asked to interview other people. I wasn't too keen on that either but some of them were enjoyable. One of these was Ireland's 'Mr Television,' Gay Byrne. I'd been after him for years for an interview. It was finally arranged through a good friend of mine, Des Duggan. He worked for the magazine *Senior Times*.

Gay proved to be very open. He regaled me with stories of how he suffered under the Christian Brothers, how he was ripped off financially by his accountant Russell Murphy, how he nearly went to Australia at one point to carve out a career there. He was also very funny. 'There were lots of letters from people urging me not go,' he said, 'It was very touching. Unfortunately, most of them were from Australia.'

I also interviewed some film stars. Often it was over the phone. That was always easier. You weren't stumped for a question and you could be scribbling away on a jotter without looking rude. Tape recorders were better of course but my one often broke down. It was a collector's item.

I used some of the material from my interviews in books I wrote afterwards. I interviewed Ned Beatty when he played Josef Locke in *Hear My Song*. In the course of our conversation he talked about how he got a part in *Network*. I used that anecdote in a book I wrote about Sidney Lumet years later.

Sometimes I got to meet the people in the flesh. The ones I remember best are Audrey Hepburn and Tony Curtis. They turned out to be more approachable than I expected. The problematic people were the ones you had to go through to get to them. Their minders acted much more like divas than they did.

Hepburn was in the early stages of cancer when I met her. She was in Ireland on a junket for Unicef. She gave a lecture about famine in Africa. At one point she showed slides of the victims. She didn't look unlike them herself. She'd always been a beanpole but looking at her now I was reminded of John Simon's description of her: 'A walking X-ray.'

Tony Curtis was just as charming. He was a rogue but a lovable one. 'The secret of eternal youth,' he once pronounced, 'is the saliva of young girls.' He was the easiest person I ever interviewed. I just turned the tape recorder on and let him go. He hardly stopped for breath for the next few hours. He also expressed a lot of interest in things I said to him. At times I felt he was interviewing me rather than the other way round. He had a great curiosity about life and people.

He talked about freebasing cocaine, about putting a gun to his head one night when he was at his lowest, about the indignities of scrambling around for work when his career went west. ('It was like I died and someone forgot to tell me.')

Now all that was behind him. He was in a good place and on a health kick. 'I don't take anything more dangerous than Diet Coke these days,' he said. After his various divorces he was also happily married. It was to a beautiful woman called Lisa Deutsch, a lawyer. She was young enough to be his daughter. 'I'd never be caught dead marrying anyone old enough to be my wife' was another one of his pronouncements.

After he went back to America he had a heart attack, Lisa left him (for two-timing) and his son committed suicide. Yes folks, this was Hollywood. Or should I say Hollyweird. Could you believe anyone? I think Tony always believed everything he said when he was saying it. He truly believed he'd be with Janet Leigh forever when he married her, and with Christine Kauffmann who came after him…and Lisa. He lived in the moment and that was good enough for him. When things changed he adapted.

Maybe that was the way with everyone in the film world. They did what felt right at the time. You only had to look at someone like Natalie Wood. She divorced Robert Wagner and then married him again. Then she divorced him a second time. Wood once appeared in a film called *The Last Married Couple in America*. A survey of the time concluded that most married couples today only talked to one another for eleven minutes a week. Dave Allen quipped, 'What do they find to talk about?'

I don't think people are as strong today as they used to be. There was a time when marriages broke up because a man beat his wife or was unfaithful to her or rolled in drunk every night looking for his sex and his supper. Today the reasons are less dramatic. I recently heard of a couple who divorced because the man liked squeezing the toothpaste from the bottom of the tube and the woman from the top. I was told it was a joke. I'm not totally sure about that.

Liz Taylor also married Richard Burton twice. Or to give her full name, Elizabeth Hilton Wilding Todd Fisher Burton Warner Fortensky. I once thought of doing a book on her. I was going to call it *The Collected Quotations*. On each page I planned to have just two words, 'I do.' The subtitle could have been *Always the Bride, Never the Bridesmaid*. I approached a few publishers with it but they turned it down. 'It's a one-joke idea,' they said - as if all books weren't that.

I bought one called *Men's Wisdom*. It consisted of 100 blank pages. I believe it went into many editions. I went through a phase of buying numerous copies of it and sending it to people I knew – all women, needless to say. They got a laugh out of it. Maybe they wouldn't have laughed quite so heartily if it was called *Women's Wisdom*. In today's '#MeToo' era you wouldn't get away with that one. My Liz Taylor book probably wouldn't have sold for the same reason. It seems you can only insult men today. Once it was the other way round. Maybe we repay the debt of history with interest.

Another person who proved to be as engaging as Curtis when I interviewed him was the writer John McGahern. He expressed great interest in anything I said to him. He wrote the story I mentioned earlier about the schoolteacher who shot an inspector when he criticised his teaching.

Like me he was from the west and like me he went to Pat's to become a teacher. He lost his job when he wrote what was called a 'dirty' book, *The Dark*. It was actually a beautiful one. He then married a Finnish woman in a registry office. You didn't do those sorts of things in the sixties and expect to get away with it, especially when a reactionary like John Charles McQuaid was the archbishop of Dublin.

The parish priest of the time famously said to McGahern, 'Why did you go off with a foreign woman when there were so many Irish ones with their tongues hanging out looking for a man?' McGahern replied dryly, 'I never noticed them turned in my direction.'

McQuaid made it his mission to get him out of the profession. He succeeded, though not before McGahern made a *cause celebre* out of the situation. He refused to go quietly. His decision exposed

various cans of worms in bureaucracy and in the way
the church ran education. McGahern went on to have
a thriving career. In time he became one of Ireland's
most famous writers - an Irish Chekhov if you like. I
showed him some of my writings when I met him.
Even a tentative word of praise from 'The Master'
made my day.

I ran into him years later in the Westbury Hotel.
He was having a drink with John Banville at the time.
I was surprised to learn they were friends. I couldn't
imagine two more opposite people. They were like an
Irish version of Hemingway and William Faulkner,
the plain-spoken man and the verbose one.

I've never been able to read Banville's books. He's
won every award under the sun but he leaves me cold.
It's as if he resents having to ground his work in any
kind of reality. *The Book of Evidence* got over that
because he used a real life backdrop for it, the story of
the killer Malcolm McArthur. The other ones always
seem too ethereal to me. Even in the Benjamin Black
books I see him as playing at being a writer instead of
being one.

I remembered reading once that Hemingway said
to Faulkner, 'Just because I don't use the ten dollar
wordsdoesn't mean I don't know them.' There's a
story told about a similar conversation that took place
between Banville and McGahern. Banville was
talking about a novel he'd just written. He was asking
his advice about it. 'I used the word "lugubrious"
twice in a paragraph,' he said to him at one stage,
'Was that a mistake?' McGahern replied in his
inimitable brogue, 'Ya shouldn't have *aiven* used it
wance.'

Leonard Cohen was another very dignified
interviewee. He was in his fifties when I met him. It
was when he was promoting his album *I'm Your Man.*
He talked about Yeats and Lorca and all the great
poets. As I listened to him I was entranced. It seemed

like a sin to be getting money to be talking to a man I'd idolised since I first heard his music. What was it about him that made him so compulsive? 'We know you're great,' a record producer said to him once, 'but are you any good?'

I knew him as a writer before I got into his songs. I'd been blown away by his novel *Beautiful Losers.* Was he one himself? 'We all are,' he said, 'merely by virtue of being alive.' Life was a losing game just as love was. Nobody emerged unscathed. As F. Scott Fitzgerald said, 'He has not lived who has not conceived life as a tragedy.'

Cohen reminded me of Fitzgerald. Hemingway said once that Fitzgerald's writing was like the dust on a butterfly's wings. It was that pure. Hemingway was more brutal.

Maybe it was like the difference between Cohen and Dylan. Which of them was the better lyricist? I couldn't say for sure. It's like comparing apples and oranges. 'Dylan is a planet,' Cohen said once, 'I just have a shop on the corner.'

They met in Paris once. They were both doing concerts there. Dylan asked Cohen how long he'd spent writing *Halleluah.* Cohen said, 'A couple of years.' It was actually seven. At one point he was banging his head off a hotel floor in his underpants trying to get the rhyme right. He asked Dylan how long he'd spent on *Just Like a Woman.* Dylan said, 'Fifteen minutes.' It was a bit like the difference between me and Harry Clifton.

Afterwards they collaborated on a song, 'Don't Go Home With Your Hard-On.' Phil Spector was the producer of it. He was the man who put a gun to Cohen's head one night when he was out of his mind with drugs. He cocked the trigger and said, 'You know I love you, don't you, Leonard?' Cohen replied, 'I hope you do, Phil, I hope you do.'

I wanted to ask him about things like this but the time was too short. Instead he talked about Hydra, about the years he spent there with Marianne Ihlen and the freewheeling atmosphere they enjoyed. His life was very simple then.

He also talked about his reputation as a depressive. I told him I never had that opinion of him. I said I found nothing more depressing than bad comedy. 'Good line,' he said.

He talked to me for almost an hour without much prompting. It was like having a chat with someone instead of doing an interview. I was hardly conscious of the tape recorder being on. He didn't seem to be either. I couldn't believe I was sitting in a room talking to Leonard Cohen. Before we finished up I gave him a book I'd written, a collection of short stories that went back to 1980. He said he was looking forward to reading it.

Afterwards I regretted not asking him about his friend Irving Layton. Layton was one of Canada's best-known poets. At that stage I didn't know how close they were to one another. My wife Mary met Layton once in the Aran Islands. In fact he wrote a poem to her. He wrote it on the back of a cigarette packet and typed it up that night, presenting it to her the next morning. It was called 'Song to Mary.' It went like this:

Willie Yeats had his Maud Gonne;
I have Mary Mannion
Who is as fair as the dawn.

Though her eyes are grey
As the break of day,
They are warm and gay.

The years will never chase
The beauty from her face
Or from her form its quiet grace.

I have come from a far land
That I may touch her hand.
O bury me in an Irish strand.

It was good to know he liked Yeats – and that he liked Mary. I was sorry I hadn't brought her with me. She liked Cohen as much as I did. She introduced me to his music when I started going round to her house first in the seventies. She thought 'Famous Blue Raincoat' was the best song he ever wrote. In fact she thought it was the best song anyone ever wrote. I didn't disagree with her.

We played his records non-stop when we started going out together. We also went to see him in concert any time we could. At that time it was only the die-hard fans who turned up at his shows. The general public seemed to be lukewarm about him. One of the clichés about his albums was that they should be have been sold with razor blades. 'Music to commit suicide by,' was the catchphrase lazy journalists used to describe it. There was a lot of cynicism about him in those days. In a way it made the concerts better that there weren't that many people at them. You felt he was singing directly to you.

When I saw him in the Point Depot years later the explosion of interest in him had taken place. Now he was public property. I felt a bit sad about that. He was more like the Pope than a pop singer. A reverential hush descended on the room whenever he spoke. Many of his songs sounded like hymns. Listening to him was as close to a religious experience as I ever got. To think I'd sat chatting with him in a little room in Jury's Hotel. Now this.

I read somewhere that as he came off the stage on one of the nights in the Point he said to his backing singer Sharon Anderson, 'I can't wait for tomorrow.' Neither could I.

I often saw him in concert in later years but I never tried to contact him again. He appeared in the grounds of the Royal Hospital in Kilmainham a few times. The audience comprised every facet of society – priests, politicians, beatnik poets. There always

158

seemed to be as much sensitivity in his audiences as there was in him. These were people who'd lived, who'd suffered. It was written all over them just like their adoration of him was written over them. 'I never felt I was God,' he said to me that day in Jury's. But sometimes it looked like it.

I didn't see him when he played two concerts at Lissadell House in Sligo in 2010. He played to over 20,000 people. It was impossible to get tickets or accommodation. The venue was a former holiday home of W.B. Yeats, his favourite poet after Lorca. I'd love to have heard him reciting the Yeats lines under Benbulben: 'The light of evening, Lissadell/Great windows open to the south/Two girls in silk kimonos/Both beautiful, one a gazelle.'

Having said that, I was never a great fan of outdoor concerts, especially where this man was concerned. The essence of Leonard Cohen was intimacy. You needed to imagine you were in a little room with him, to have the sounds bouncing back off the walls. I once installed a sound system in my house just to play his records. When I turned the woofer on I could feel the sounds coming up through my shoes.

I bought every album he ever recorded right down to the last one, 'You Want it Darker.' The title was probably an example of him being mischievous. It was like an acknowledgement that the people who said he was depressing were right after all. He was finally having fun with his image.

Should it have been sold with razor blades? No. There was nothing as depressing as bad comedy.

Cohen died in 2015. He hadn't been well for a number of years. He'd been rolling along so long you tended to forget his age. I was shocked to learn he was older than Elvis.

In July of that year a friend of his former lover Marianne Ihlen wrote to him to say that Marianne was dying of cancer. She was the woman pictured on the iconic cover of his album 'Songs from a Room.' She was sitting at his typewriter with a towel wrapped around her. His reply went viral on social media.

'Dearest Marianne,' he said, 'I'm just a little behind you, close enough to take your hand. This old body had given up just as yours has. I've never forgotten your love or your beauty. Safe travels, old friend. See you down the road.'

She was the Marianne of 'So Long Marianne' and the influence behind many other songs he wrote, like 'Bird on the Wire.' She gave him that line after looking out the window one day and seeing a bird sitting on the wire of a telegraph pole. Electrification had just come to Hydra.

There'd been many 'so longs' over the years. After spending most of the sixties with her on the island he left her to go back to his other life, that of the writer-cum-singer in America. He sent her tickets for his concerts over the years but they were scant consolation to her.

She didn't take the parting well. Their relationship had been so pure during the magic decade of the sixties when everyone was dropping out to find themselves. She thought it was going to last forever among the artistic colony they mixed with. But Cohen couldn't be pinned down. His mind was always elsewhere. Neither was Marianne creative. She was more of a support structure to artists like Cohen and her former lover, the novelist Axel Jensen.

She crumbled after he left her. She'd put the son she'd had by Jensen into Suffolk's progressive Summerhill school to give her some breathing space but he hadn't done well there. In time she went back to her native Norway to live. She married there in 1979 and settled down to an old-fashioned life.

I met some more famous people after Cohen. Editors often asked me if I wanted to interview actors and musicians who were passing through Dublin.

When the opportunity came to meet Emmylou Harris I jumped at it.

There were times I felt I could happily spend the rest of my life listening to Emmylou – and looking at her. Maybe there should have been a law against looking that good. And sounding that good.

Meeting her fell below my expectations. Maybe she was tired on the night in question or maybe she was just too cerebral a creature to engage in small talk. It was after one of her shows in the National Concert Hall. In retrospect I think I must have been tongue-tied. Her road manager Phil Kaufman was also there. He was the man who stole Gram Parsons' body from a mortuary after he died so he could cremate it in the Mojave desert. He stopped anything happening between us.

She had a poignance in her that night that made me think she'd be an ideal candidate for singing Bob Dylan's epic song 'Sad-Eyed Lady of the Lowlands.' Joan Baez had covered it movingly on her Dylan album 'Love is Just a Four-Lettered Word' some years before. Maybe it's better that she wasn't upbeat when I spoke to her. It meant I could preserve the emotion I usually had when I listened to her: heartbreak. I always preferred her melancholy songs to her sassy ones.

I also met another beautiful woman at this time, the actress Angie Dickinson. She was friendlier than Emmylou by far. It was after a showing of the film *Rio Bravo* in the Irish Film Institute one day. I told her I'd love to write her life story with her. Had she any plans in that regard? 'If I ever do it,' she said, 'I'll do it myself.'

To date she hasn't. I feel she has a lot to tell. Maybe she's not the type to, or maybe too much of it hurts too much. Like Emmylou Harris, her love life hasn't been exactly idyllic. Why does this always seem to be the case with beautiful women? Angie also

161

lost a daughter to suicide. This is something else that seems to assail famous people all too frequently. It also happened to Tony Curtis, Paul Newman, Gregory Peck and Mary Tyler Moore.

Another pretty woman I interviewed was the singer Juliet Turner. I went through a phase of being mesmerised by her voice, especially on songs like 'Burn the Black Suit.' She too failed to live up to expectations when I talked to her. I found myself having to drag the answers to my questions out of her. When the interview appeared in print I rang her to tell her about it, only to hear her say, 'I don't read my interviews.'

I couldn't believe my ears. It was so different to people like John McGahern and Leonard Cohen who were infinitely bigger talents and unfailingly polite to me. Where's Juliet Turner today? Nowhere, I suspect. I can't help feeling it's poetic justice. The smaller the talent, it often seems, the bigger the ego.

John McEnroe wasn't overly friendly either. I met him one year at a GOAL event. He wasn't pleased when I interrupted a conversation he was having with another tennis player, Mats Wilander, to ask him for his autograph. I now knew how referees felt when he looked at them and said, 'You cannot be serious.'

Another person who wasn't exactly bubbling over with friendliness was Charlton Heston, especially when I picked him up on a typo that was in his autobiography. It was in Eason's one day at a signing session. You didn't do that to Moses without incurring his wrath. Maybe I was lucky he didn't strike me with a tablet of stone. I'd remembered Richard Harris saying of him once, 'Chuck is so square he could drop out of a cubic moon.' They'd fallen out on the set of a film they made. Heston didn't like Harris' unpunctuality and told him so.

Harris took to arriving with dozens of clocks around his shoulders.

Experiences like the one with Heston made me realise it was important to keep the worlds of journalism and fandom apart. It was a lesson I had to learn the hard way. Some people seemed to know it instinctively. Keith worshipped the stars of Hollywood but he never expressed much of an interest in meeting them, not even his hero James Cagney when he came to Ireland to shoot *Shake Hands with the Devil*.

I was a different animal. If I ever saw anyone famous in the street I almost had to be physically restrained from going up to them. I approached John Boorman in a hotel one day simply because a girl I was with at the time dared me to. I liked Boorman's work but he wasn't a hero of mine. I just wanted to respond to the dare.

It was only after the experience of being underwhelmed by celebrities that I changed. It made me think about them differently. I enjoyed meeting people like Jimmy White but I'm not too sure if I'd like to have run into some of my other heroes. Robert De Niro, for instance. From what I've seen of him in interviews I don't think he'd exactly be Dale Carnegie. The same applies to Bob Dylan. Like De Niro, he doesn't seem to suffer fools – or fans – gladly.

Flaubert said never meet your idols. The gilt rubbed off on your fingers. I don't know if there's any truth to the story that a fan of Samuel Beckett saw him sitting outside a café in Paris one day and went up to him.

'What are you thinking about?' the fan said. Beckett is alleged to have replied, 'I'm waiting for Gateaux.'

There's a similar story told about a woman who was a fan of the actor Richard Gere. She wanted to go to bed with him and was willing to go to any lengths to bring this about.

She got close to his security guard to see if she could make it happen. The security guard slept with her. Her friend met her the next morning and asked her if she'd enjoyed it. 'It was okay,' she said, 'but it wasn't like sleeping with Richard.'

Afterwards she made friends with his limousine driver and slept with him too. Her friend asked her how that went. 'It was okay,' she said, 'but it wasn't like sleeping with Richard.'

Finally she met the man himself. She was so excited she couldn't think straight. A room was booked in a hotel in Las Vegas and the deed was done.

She met her friend again the next morning. When she asked her how it went she said, 'It was okay, but it wasn't like sleeping with Richard.'

Sixteen

The next two books I wrote had a common theme. They were both biographies, one of Sidney Lumet and the other of Marlon Brando. Brando was directed by Lumet in *The Fugitive Kind*. Their paths crossed some years earlier when Brando was a stage actor. After he left the play *A Flag is Born* on Broadway his shoes were filled by Lumet. Lumet was an actor before he became a director.

That was the first book I wrote about a director. One of the reasons I did it was because nobody had done a biography of him before. Shortly after it came out I learned that another writer, Maura Spiegel, had just written one. It was a weird coincidence. Both of us were claiming on Amazon that ours was 'the first' biography of Lumet. I wasn't aware she was doing her book until I saw it on the shelves. She probably didn't know about mine either.

Maybe it wasn't that weird. Every second person in the world seemed to think they had a book in them. What right had I to think someone wouldn't invade my little patch? My father used to say, 'There's nothing new under the sun.' Maybe he was right. Brian Behan had a more earthy way of putting it. 'We're all pissing in the same pot,' he'd say anytime we discussed writing.

Many people wrote biographies of Brando. To make my one different I chose what I thought was a unique aspect of him – his humour. It was published by a company called Propertius Press. Like Ken Clay, the editor was a writer herself. Her name was Susannah Eanes. She'd published some Deep South novels in the style of Eudora Welty.

I promised myself I'd do something on Brando for years but I hadn't got around to it until now. I liked him just as much as I liked Elvis. They had a lot in common. They were both country boys. Both of them had alcoholic parents, both of them idolised their mothers and both were alienated from their fathers. Both of them were also fair-haired men who preferred brunette women to any other kind. Both of them got obese in their later years, both revolutionised the fifties, went soft in the sixties, and had their renaissance in the seventies. Elvis idolised Brando but for Brando Elvis' success owned 'more to myth than magnificence.'

I'd planned to see Elvis in 1972 when I was in Connecticut but it fell through. I wanted to see Brando when he came here to film *Divine Rapture* in 1995 but that didn't work out either. He was playing a priest in the film. Apparently he'd had great fun on it with Johnny Depp. He'd become friendly with him a few years beforehand during the shooting of another film, *Don Juan de Marco.* It was being filmed in Ballycotton, County Cork. Audrey lived nearby. I could have stayed with her and commuted but after a few scenes were shot the money ran out. There were no backers forthcoming so everyone went home. *Divine Rapture* became *Divine Rupture.* I was devastated. So was Depp. He said it was like being interrupted in the middle of good sex.

Brando was sad too even though he'd got his fee upfront, unlike Depp and the other members of the cast. Before he left Ireland he was photographed standing at the window of the mansion he was staying in. He was wearing nothing but his briefs in the shot. His gigantic stomach tumbled out over them. It was a very intrusive photograph taken from a sleazy journalist with a long lens camera.

Brando was always self-conscious about his weight. The photo ended his honeymoon with Ireland. Up to now he'd been talking fondly about it. He even suggested he might take up Irish citizenship at one point. He liked its unpretentiousness. It reminded him of his magical Tetiaroa, the atoll he'd bought off

166

Tahiti after filming *Mutiny on the Bounty*. That idyll ended when his son killed his daughter's fiancé there in 1994. Now another one was over.

My focus in the book was on his tendency towards mischief. There'd been many books written on 'brooding Brando.' I wanted to bring out his other side. He'd been playing pranks on people since childhood. He never stopped, even when he was in his seventies.

He'd been a big thing in my life from the Ballina days. I was too young to have seen the great fifties films when they came out but I caught up with them later, viewing many of them many times. He threatened to retire from acting when Martin Luther King was shot in 1968. Films were never as important to him as social issues. He was about to re-unite with Elia Kazan that year for a film called *The Arrangement.* I'd been looking forward to seeing it. Now he dropped out, something he did a lot during his career. Kirk Douglas got the part instead and butchered it.

Brando made some interesting films in the seventies but he didn't do much after that. The critics made fun of him more often than not. I went to every bad film he made. That was what a fan was, wasn't it? Someone who even likes your bad stuff? If he had ten good seconds in a film that made the admission price worth it for me. It could be something as small as the way he raised an eyebrow or looked at someone. I asked for no more.

He kept threatening to retire. Why was it that so many of the people I liked in life wanted to retire young? Ronnie O' Sullivan was the most obvious example but there were others. Bjorn Borg walked away from tennis after his five-year winning run ended at Wimbledon ended in 1981. I also thought Steffi Graf retired too young. It was in 1999. She was thirty at the time but she was still number 3 in the world. She'd also reached a Wimbledon final that year.

Graf was my favourite tennis player after McEnroe. I could watch her delivering those cross-court backhand volleys forever. When I got interested in someone I always took it badly when they lost. So it was with her. Monica Seles started to beat her repeatedly at one stage of her career. I couldn't stand Seles' grunting. Peter Ustinov said, 'God help the neighbours on her wedding night.'

Was there any way Graf could stop her? There didn't seem to be but fate took a hand in 1993. That was the year Seles was stabbed between the shoulder blades by a demented fan called Gunther Parche. Why had he done it? So Graf could regain her number 1 ranking position.

I don't condone violence but I was over the moon after it happened. He was a man after my own heart. I hadn't kept my feelings about Seles to myself over the years. For a while I thought I was going to be the prime suspect for putting him up to it. I expected a knock on the door any day and a burly sergeant saying to me, 'Are you acquainted with Gunther Parche?'

Why couldn't someone have stabbed Steve Davis when he was beating Jimmy White? Or Ray Reardon when he was beating Alex Higgins?

Graf won 65 of the next 67 matches she played. Seles was out of action for two years. That was as much from the psychological trauma as the injury. Graf beat her in the US Open when she came back on the tour. Everything looked rosy for me for a while but then she started losing. She was also beset by injuries and tax problems. Every time I liked someone there seemed to be complications in their lives.

Who was left now? Who'd surprise me by not retiring?

Ronnie O'Sullivan came on the snooker scene around now. He blew everyone away when he turned professional. He replaced Jimmy White for me just as Jimmy had replaced Alex Higgins. There always seemed to be a new icon for me to love in snooker. It was as if the gods were timing it.

But the gods also injected a flaw into my heroes. Ronnie was famous for his threats to retire from snooker. I think he made the first one when he was in nappies. I remembered him walking out on a match with Hendry when he was only 3-1 down. He shook his hand after missing a red and abruptly departed the building.

Ronnie won the world championship in 2001 and 2004. In 2005 he lost the quarter-final to Peter Ebdon after holding a good lead. I had to leave the match in the middle and press the 'Record' button. It clashed with the launch of a book I'd just written, a biography of Malachy Smyth, the pioneering back surgeon. That was in Castle Leslie, a luxurious hotel in Monaghan. Paul McCartney had married Heather Mills there the previous year. I was there to launch my book on Malachy Smyth. I had to give a lecture on it to a team of surgeons. They attending an official event. A pharmacist was launching a new tablet that had just come on the market.

Giving a lecture to a roomful of medical experts would have been difficult at the best of times. It was a hundred times worse on the night in question because I kept wondering how Ronnie was doing as I spoke. I looked down at the sea of eminent faces. They looked back at me with an expression that seemed to say, 'Educate us.' I felt I was in some kind of a surreal movie.

I used a lot of big words to try and pretend I knew what I was talking about but they didn't look too impressed. When you stand in front of fifty consultants and the only medical text you've ever consulted in your life was the day you were looking for a cure for a nosebleed when you were twelve you don't exactly feel qualified to talk about the finer points of spinal surgery. One man left the hall when I was in mid-sentence.I felt like joining him. I think he was going to the bar.

I couldn't stop thinking of Ronnie. As I was driving back to Dublin the next morning a news report came on the radio. Ebdon had beaten him. He caught up with him by playing at snail's pace and trapping him in some of those endless bouts of safety for which he was renowned. There was only going to be one winner in that scenario. He knew Ronnie would snap sooner or later and start playing kamikaze snooker.

I felt it wouldn't have happened if I'd been there to watch it. Sometimes I believed my karma could guide him along. I'd be roaring at the television screen like I used to do with Jimmy. Malachy Smyth knocked that possibility on the head.

Losing the match was bad enough but the radio report said Ronnie was frustrated with his game and considering retiring. Why hadn't I stayed in Dublin? Who cared about a stupid book?

The first thing I did when I got home was turn on the television to see the recording of the match. There was more heartache there. The tape didn't come out. It played an Ard-Fheis speech by Bertie Ahern instead. The soundtrack was of the snooker but the picture was of Ahern. I've never had that experience before or since. Was it Ebdon's gremlins that scuppered my tape? Had these caused ronnie's lead to ebb away?

He held an even better lead against Mark Selby in the world final of 2014 but he still managed to lose it. I made a lot of money on that match, backing Selby to win when he was way behind. By now I never took anything for granted with Ronnie. I got Selby at 7/1 and put 100 euro on him.

I didn't see the end of the match. It clashed with a wedding I'd been invited to. One of Mary's friends from the crèche she worked in was getting married. We went to it but my mind was a million miles away. I couldn't concentrate on the wedding any more than I'd been able to concentrate on my speech in Castle Leslie in 2005 when I was launching my biography of Malachy Smyth. Snooker always seemed to interrupt things I was doing in my life.

I sped home from the wedding to catch a bit of Ronnie's match but then we had to leave again for the reception. I couldn't concentrate on that either. I left it at one point to see what was happening on the television in the bar downstairs. Selby was catching up on him, catching up on him the way Steve Davis used to catch up on Jimmy White, the way Cliff Thorburn used to catch up on Alex Higgins. These players were spiders. They waited in the long grass for my heroes to make a mistake. Then they pounced on them.

Mary came down after me. 'Everyone is looking for you,' she said. I said, 'Selby is going to beat him. My life is over.'

That's what happened. It was the first world final he'd lost. He threatened to retire again afterwards.

I went back to the reception but I couldn't get into the swing of it. Mary didn't know what was wrong with me.

'I thought you put money on Selby,' she said.

'I did,' I said 'but it's no good to me.'

'I don't understand.'

It was too complicated to explain I knew I had to get out of there.

We told the bride the car was acting up, that we had to go home. If they knew the truth they'd have thought I was crazy. Maybe I was.

I'd met Selby years before in my local bowling alley in Coolock. It was by accident. I'd gone in to get some change for a phone call. He was playing video games with Neil Robertson and Barry Hawkins.

It was in the early days of his career. He hadn't done much yet. I told him to keep plugging away at it, that one day it would come right for him. I was annoyed with myself afterwards for encouraging him. I had no idea then that he'd win three world titles or be such a thorn in Ronnie's side.

He always took a particular delight in beating Ronnie. It was like a cause. He seemed to be jealous of his natural talent and made it his business to do him down.

Selby's nickname is 'The Jester from Leicester.' Snooker nicknames derive either from rhymes like this one or alliteration like Hurricane Higgins, Whirlwind White or Rocket Ronnie. Selby's one doesn't make much sense. He's about as funny as a heart attack.

He went on to win three world titles. I went through torture watching all three of them. He became even more of a hate figure to me than Davis was. If he went out of a tournament early it put me into good form even if Ronnie had been beaten too. As I got older I took more pleasure in the defeat of my enemies than the victories of my friends. My friends tended to win less than my enemies.

Why couldn't I make boring people my heroes? Why couldn't I follow someone like Selby or Robertson - or John Higgins, a man who was as different from Alex Higgins as it was possible to be. They aren't related.

Why did I have to develop an attachment to someone like Brando in the acting world? It meant I had to endure him baling out of projects or not giving his best to the when he fell out of love with acting? Why couldn't I have followed someone like Bill

172

Roache in *Coronation Street*? As I write, Bill is appearing in his 10,285th episode of *Corrie*. He must have started it in a previous life. They've even put him in a nursing home. They'll probably film him as he's dribbling into his soup at 108.

Where does that leave us? With a system of communications that has less culture than yoghurt, maybe, being presided over by people with IQs somewhere below room temperature.

There are very few 'characters' left in the world today. Where are the Brendan Behans, the Flann O'Briens? The modern author sips spring water and goes to conventions instead of getting maggoty drunk in McDaids.

There are few characters in sport either. I can't see anyone like Muhammad Ali, the boxer my mother loved. He had the audacity to say, 'I'm the greatest.' In darts we had Eric Bristow. In tennis we had Ilie Nastase and John McEnroe. I liked Seve Ballesteros for his ability to get into trouble and then to get out of it. Jimmy White was another Houdini. Who's replaced these people and so many others now gone for their tea? Automatons.

Sometimes the people themselves become automatons. Jimmy went soft many years ago. McEnroe became a friend of Donald Trump.

When Alex Higgins met Stephen Hendry at a snooker match once he said to him, 'Hello, I'm the devil.' It was after he'd threatened Dennis Taylor's life when they had a bust-up. It's hard to imagine something like that happening today.

The modern world is bland. Everything is stratified, right down to vacuum-packed food and microwave ovens. You see the same thing in the world of art, of music. I don't think we'll have many Beethovens in the future, just more people like Bill Gates and Mark Zuckerberg.

Where do we go from here? I wish I knew the answer to that. People's lives will continue to become more compartmentalised. They'll do their forty hours work every week and then retreat to caves in suburbia to drink Prosecco and watch Netflix. They'll stare into their phones instead of communicating with one another. They'll leave towns like Ballina for cities like Dublin in search of thrills, spills and the next high.

Or maybe just somewhere to hang their hat.

Seventeen

Another book I wrote recently was a revamp of one I'd done a few years ago called *And the Loser Is*. It was a study of all the people who'd never won Oscars. Great actors like Montgomery Clift and Peter O'Toole and many others never got one. I felt they'd be more interesting than the winners. There'd been dozens of books written on these.

Often the wrong people won. They were given the award for service or for playing someone with a terminal disease or for sentimental reasons or simply for hanging around long enough. Sometimes the winners were losers too. Their careers often went bad after their victory. So did their personal lives.

I tried to make the book into a capsule history of Hollywood. It was my chance to say everything I felt about that crazy town. When I started it I told Keith about my ambition with it. I was looking forward to him seeing it between covers but he died before it was published. I'm not sure if he would have liked it. He generally agreed with the Academy's decisions on Oscars. My brief was to debunk them all.

Did he believe the Academy was right to give Humphrey Bogart the Oscar in 1951 (for *The African Queen*) instead of Marlon Brando for *A Streetcar Named Desire*? Probably. Did he believe they were right to give one to John Wayne in 1969 for *True Grit* instead of Dustin Hoffman for *Midnight Cowboy*? Probably.

I once told him I was thinking of doing a book on The Hollywood Ten. This was the group of people who were blacklisted in Hollywood for left-wing affiliations. He said, 'Yes, it was a terrible time.' I thought he meant because of the way they were treated but it was the opposite of that. He believed it

175

was bad because of the threat they posed to the establishment.

When I told him I was doing my M.A. thesis on Hemingway he said, 'Why didn't you pick Scott Fitzgerald?' It was the old wedding/funeral scenario again. Fitzgerald was the wedding, Hemingway the funeral.

We were like chalk and cheese. That didn't mean either of us was superior to the other. In some ways I was relieved he wasn't alive when the book came out. It would have upset him too much to see me trashing so many of his sacred cows.

My thesis about winners suffering from the Oscar 'curse' got more credibility when I looked into the life of Gig Young. He won a Best Supporting Actor award for the film *They Shoot Horses, Don't They?* in 1969. Years later he shot himself and his young fiancé in a murder/suicide that shocked the world.

Despite being years after his victory, his first wife said he'd started to go downhill after winning. The part was tragic and so was he. Even when he smiled he looked sad. In the film he was the MC of a marathon dance competition. Most of the contestants looked as if they could have done with a phone call to the Samaritans.

Maybe victory and defeat are really two sides of the one coin. My father liked to quote Omar Khayaam's *If*.

His favourite lines in it were, 'If you can meet with fortune and disaster/and treat those two imposters just the same.' 'Imposters' was an interesting word in the context. I thought about my book in the same way. You lost whether you won or lost.

I emailed the cover of it to an editor I worked for, John Low of *Senior Times*. It was a magazine I was doing some articles for at the time. He used to advise me about the covers of my books. His specialty was graphic design. He said, 'You'd want to watch the spacing.' I didn't know what he meant until I looked at it again.

He was right. My name was too close to the title of the book. You could have looked at it and thought the name of it was *And the Loser Is Aubrey Malone.* I'm sure my enemies would have liked that. Maybe there was a Freudian slip in it. I contacted the editor and asked him to widen it.

In the end maybe it's all down to character. That's what Jackie Gleason said to Paul Newman when he played Eddie Felson in *The Hustler.* You might be born with a great talent but if you don't have the character to back it up it mightn't go anywhere. From this point of view, snooker spills over into the way we think about life in general.

Why is sport so important to us? Is it because, as T.S. Eliot said, humankind cannot bear too much reality? I prefer to see it is a higher form of reality rather than an escape from it. It's a symbol of who we aspire to be. It defines us in a way life doesn't, both in our highest versions of ourselves and our Achilles heels.

Maybe Mayo will never win an All-Ireland again. Maybe I'll never get over Creeper. These things are hardwired into our DNA. It's what coming from the west of Ireland means. We form obsessions we can't outgrow. Or maybe we don't want to.

Jimmy White, Creeper, Mayo, me – we're all losers. We're like Shane and Elvis and Hemingway and Leonard Cohen and F. Scott Fitzgerald and Marlon Brando in *On the Waterfront.* Each of us is on a one-way ticket to Palookaville. We have what Shakespeare called a *hamartia* – a fatal flaw.

Jimmy was the bridesmaid at six Sheffield weddings. Cohen wore defeat like a second skin. Fitzgerald died at 44 as a has-been. Brando struggled on till eighty but he didn't do anything worthwhile for the last twenty years of his life.

177

Creeper and myself fell into jobs we didn't want because they were the only things open to us. Mayo couldn't win the All-Ireland because of a curse. Not one that was put on them by a priest but rather by themselves.

Losers may not be attractive to someone when they come to them looking for help but from a romantic perspective they knock the socks off winners. There's a cavalcade of them in Hollywood's back pages. You only have to think of someone like Frank Sinatra singing 'Here's to the Losers.'

Maybe I should have put Sinatra on the cover of this book. He epitomises the theme of the loser to a T, both in his life and career. When he was dating Ava Gardner in the early fifties his career hit an all-time low. He couldn't give his records away for free. At one stage he considered ending it all. Everything changed after Gardner made a phone call to the wife of Harry Cohn, the producer of *From Here to Eternity*. It resulted in him getting an Oscar for his performance in that film. Today we look on Sinatra as a success story but when I listen to him singing 'Here's to the Losers,' or when I see the video of him singing 'One For the Road' at a quarter to three in the morning I can see the other side of the coin.

Was my father a loser because he never realised his dream of becoming a State solicitor? John Lennon said once, 'A part of me suspects I'm a loser and a part suspects I'm God Almighty.' That was my father too. He could veer from one image of himself to the other. Maybe all fantasists do that on different days – or even on the same day. The man waiting on Flight 1203 was a loser too – in love. Maybe that's the worst kind of one to be.

Hemingway was a loser as well. 'The world breaks everyone,' he said, 'and many are strong at the broken places.' He had many of these. They got worse as the years went on. At the end of his life he'd lost both his talent and his mind. When there was nothing left to lose he shot himself. One of his books was called *Winner Take Nothing*. That was a subtheme of my book on the Oscars. Maybe it was a subtheme of them all.

My fascination with Hollywood's dark side was another example of that. Marilyn Monroe overdosing on Seconal in the middle of her last phone call. James Dean breaking his neck on a Cholame highway. Elvis getting a coronary in a Memphis bathroom.

Would I have continued reading about these people if they lived to ripe old ages? I don't know. It wasn't that I wished ill on them. It was more the fact that you couldn't say anything about survival except that it happened. There was no story behind it. The stories were behind loss, devastation, the slow decline into oblivion. If Brando hadn't had to throw a fight in *On the Waterfront* there would have been no story either. If Shane was allowed to stay in the Wyoming valley there would have been no story. Stories come from failure, fate, entrapment.

Religion loves losers too. Satan was a more interesting character than God in *Paradise Lost*. Judas was a more interesting one than Jesus in *Jesus Christ Superstar*. One of the most beloved saints in Christendom is St. Jude of Hopeless Cases.

Was Bukowski a loser? He thought everyone was. Sooner or later, he said, life burns us. It burns us in our family and our jobs and everything else. We never get what we want and then it ends.

Anyone reading this book might see it as an inventory of failure. That isn't its intention. It never bothered me that I couldn't play snooker as well as the other people in the club I was in or that I couldn't teach as well as the other teachers in my school or sing as well as the people in the singing pubs or play tennis like John McEnroe. The point is that I tried.

Most of the people in these worlds never ventured outside them. When I inhabited them I met connoisseurs. One man I used to play in the snooker hall insisted on washing the balls before we played. Many teachers I worked with acted as if the world would stop if their pupils didn't know their ABCs. I knew tennis players who got up at dawn to work on their volleys.

I could never have that kind of discipline. I preferred to model myself on someone like Ferdinand Waldo Demara, the character played by Tony Curtis in *The Great Imposter*. Demara performed major chest surgery on people during the Korean War despite having no medical training. I didn't quite go that far in Castle Leslie when I lectured to consultants about spine surgery. But I got a smattering of what it must have felt like.

'Why don't you concentrate more on what you're good at?' My mother's words came back to me. I didn't know the answer to her question when she put it to me but I do now. It's because being good at things bores me.

Robert Mitchum's wife used to say that he could spend a weekend fixing a hinge on a door. I could spend a week doing that.

I don't own a drill. When we needed a grab rail in the shower I tied a piece of rope from the towel rail onto the soap stand. I wrapped duct tape over it about fifty times to secure it.

There's a drawer in the kitchen that has about a hundred nails in it. It was coming loose so I hammered them all in. A skilled craftsman could have sorted out the problem with two. It looks like it's been riddled with bullets. That doesn't bother me. It isn't loose anymore. That's all that matters.

I have briquettes under the floorboards in the attic to prevent the passage of mice through them. When people go up there they ask me what they're for. I say, 'I like setting the floor on fire sometimes. It creates a nice atmosphere.'

I enjoyed doing jobs like that more than I enjoyed writing. There were times I thought I'd have preferred to have gone to the Tech in Ballina rather than Muredach's. Clive said to me once, 'That's not who you are.' I understood why he said it. It was like my mother advising me to stick to what I was good at. Neither of them understood me. I preferred doing what I was bad at. There was more of a challenge in it.

Jimmy White often expended his energy creating the most perfect opportunities for himself in snooker games by some incredible play. Then he missed a sitter. Why? Because the challenge was over. The easy ones bored him. I could identify with that.

I could have been a better singer if I sang in a lower key. There was no challenge in that either. It's only when your voice cracks that you know you've taken it to the limit. I always liked taking things to their limits. Isn't that what the Peter Principle is – rising to your level of incompetence? It worked for this Peter anyway.

It extended to my work too. I could have been a more successful teacher if I tightened up my discipline and stopped getting familiar with the pupils. Why didn't I? Maybe I felt that wouldn't have worked either. It would have turned me into the person I'd been when I was a pupil myself, a cog in the machine.

I never got to the top in the writing world because I didn't cosy up to the right people. I stayed away from the society parties. I didn't put self-promotion before the job in hand. That would have been another kind of selling out.

Marlon Brando once said the film most people asked him about in his life was *On the Waterfront*. The reason was because he played a loser in it.

'Everyone could identify with that,' he claimed. It was only when Steve Davis started to lose at snooker that he developed the kind of fanbase previously only accorded to 'bad boys' like Jimmy White and Alex Higgins. People were gratified to know he was human after all.

Winners, losers, what's the difference? In many ways they're two sides of the same coin. We can't appreciate victory until we've tasted defeat. Maybe one leads inexorably to the other. It's a station along the way, a blooding of ourselves that makes us real. We have to stare into the abyss before we see the light.

Jesus did that. He was a loser too, at least on the surface of things. The church celebrates his resurrection but not before it reminds us what he had to do to attain it. As Martin Scorsese said of the Catholic religion, 'Too much Good Friday and not enough Easter Sunday.'

Defeat is more educational than victory. We learn nothing from success except for the fact that we enjoy it. Is it fulfilling? Some people look on it as the end of the road, the last step on a journey that can go no further. When you climb the mountain, what is there to do but go back down again? Realise all your dreams and there's nothing left. Do you rest on your laurels or look for new ones?

Some more lines from *The Rubaiyat* come back to me:

'If you can make one heap of all your winnings
And risk it on one turn of pitch and toss,
And lose, and start again from the beginning,
And never breathe a word about your loss.'

How many of us can do that? Could my father? I think of his faded grandeur, of Hemingway's grace under pressure, of Jimmy White – a noble savage going into the Crucible year after year and leaving it with nothing except his pride. Was that enough? To be the People's Champion rather than the Champion proper?

People embrace fallibility in politics in the same way as they do in sport. Bill Clinton escaped the ultimate censure with Monica Lewinsky just like John F. Kennedy did with Marilyn Monroe in a previous era. When somebody falls on their sword, like Lance Armstrong did on the Oprah Winfrey show, people empathise with them. We've all been that soldier.

Even if we're losers there's always a way back for us, especially if we've paid the price. Sometimes that price is a debt to society. Sometimes it's a debt to ourselves.

Maybe at the end of the day it's a question of attitude. You can see chicken shit and call it chicken salad. You can see mud and call it magic. You can see Donald Trump and think John F. Kennedy.

The world moves on. We fall and we rise. We cry and then laugh. We sin and seek forgiveness. At one time the forgiveness was presided over by the church. Today the psychologists have supplanted them. Talking heads on our media have replaced the cloistered figures of yore.

Whatever our problem is today, we can get a spin doctor to get us out of it, or a PR person or a fixer. Afterwards, we know, the world will love us even more. Because that's what the world does. It embraces losers.

People see themselves in losers because we're all sinners, we've all lost our way, we've all fallen three times under the cross.

Why was Ben Dunne forgiven for his cocaine and hooker scandal in the 1990s? Because he said 'Mea culpa.' When Clinton was asked why he had sex with Lewinsky he said, 'Why did Adam eat the apple?' It goes back that far. Adam and Eve were the first losers, literally eating themselves out of house and home. Their descendants have been picking up the slack ever since.

'Show me a good loser,' said Paul Newman, 'and I'll show you a loser.' He would know. Eddie Felson would too. Because he lacked character. We like winners because they're always celebrating but losers are more interesting.

They also make better subjects for books.